dan j. marlowe
the name of the game is death

Dan J. Marlowe was born in Lowell, Massachusetts, in
1914. His crime novels and short stories have appeared
in more than a dozen countries and languages and he
won the Edgar Allan Poe Award from the Mystery
Writers of America. He died in Los Angeles in 1987.

the name of the game is death

dan j. marlowe

VINTAGE CRIME / **BLACK LIZARD**

vintage books • a division of random house, inc. • new york

First Vintage Crime/Black Lizard Edition, May 1993

Library of Congress Cataloging-in-Publication Data
Marlowe, Dan J., 1914–1987
The name of the game is death/by Dan J. Marlowe.
— 1st Vintage Crime/Black Lizard ed.
p.   cm.—(Vintage Crime/Black Lizard)
ISBN 0-679-73848-7
I. Title.   II. Series.
PS3563.A67395N34   1993
813'.54—dc20   92-50690   CIP

Manufactured in the United States of America
10 9 8 7 6 5 4 3

the name of the game is death

1

From the back seat of the Olds I could see the kid's cotton gloves flash white on the steering wheel as he swung off Van Buren onto Central Avenue. On the right up ahead the strong late September Phoenix sunshine blazed off the bank's white stone front till it hurt the eyes. The damn building looked as big as the purple buttes on the rim of the desert.

Beside me Bunny chewed gum rhythmically, his hands relaxed in his lap. Up front, in three-quarter profile the kid's face was like chalk, but he teamed the car perfectly into a tight-fitting space right in front of the bank.

Nobody said a word. I climbed out on the sidewalk side, and Bunny got out opposite and walked around the rear to join me. His dark glasses and bright yellow hair glinted in the sun. The thick, livid scar across his throat was nearly hidden in his week-old beard. Across the street the big clock said five minutes to three. Under it on another dial a long thermometer needle rested on ninety-four. A shirt-sleeved man stood idly beneath the clock.

We crossed the sidewalk and passed through the bank's outer glass doors. I'm five ten, but Bunny towered over me six inches. I could see the rolled-up canvas sack under his arm. In the vestibule the air conditioning bit hard at the sweat on my face and arms. Bunny led the way through into the main floor lobby. He went left. I went right. Two guards on the main floor.

I found my guard showing an old man how to fill out a deposit slip. I moved in behind the guard, and when I saw Bunny's arm go up across the way I slammed the red-creased neck in front of me with a solid chunk of Smith & Wesson. He went down without a sound. The old man kept right on writing. I heard a choked gurgle from Bunny's guard. That was all.

I took my first good look around while I switched to the Colt Woodsman. If we hadn't gotten those two, we were nowhere. A dozen to fifteen customers, scattered. I fired the Woodsman three times, taking out glass high in the tellers' cages each time. Shattering glass is an impressive sound. In the echoing lobby the glass and the little Woodsman sounded like a turret of sixteen-inchers in a china closet.

"All right, everybody," I said, loud and clear. "Everybody stand still and nobody gets hurt."

Nobody moved. Nobody breathed. Bunny vaulted the low gate up in front. I jammed the Woodsman back in my pants, and balanced the Smith & Wesson again in my palm. If somebody fast-pitched us, I might need the three heavier caliber bullets I'd saved by directing traffic with the Woodsman.

Inside the railing with Bunny, two big-assed women huddled together against the door leading into the cages, empty trays in their hands. Right where they should have been at two minutes to three. Bunny motioned with his gun at the cage door. They stared at him, cow-eyed. Inside the cages there wasn't a sound. Bunny whipped the flat of his automatic up against the jawline of the nearer woman. She fell over sideways, mewling. Someone inside opened the door. Bunny stepped in quickly, herding everyone to the rear. He began yanking out cash drawers. Bundles of hundreds and twenties went into the sack. Everything else went to the floor.

The only thing I could hear was the whimpering of the woman on the floor and the clatter and bang as Bunny emptied and dumped drawers. On my left something moved. I turned, and the movement stopped. Dead ahead on the balcony overhead I caught a rapid blur of gray. I belted the guard over backward with the first shot I banged up there. Bunny never even turned his head.

Two minutes, I'd figured, after we took out the first guards. Two and a half, tops. All over town now bells would be ringing, but in sixty seconds we'd be gone. I did a slow turn, eyes skimming the balcony and the main floor. Nothing.

Bunny burst out the cage door, hugging the sack to his

big chest. He jumped the railing, landing on his toes. I fell in six feet behind him, and we went out through the vestibule at a fast walk. Bunny had just reached out to open the right hand outer glass door when there was a sharp crack-crack-crack from behind us. The best part of the door blew right out onto the sidewalk. Heat rolled in through the splintered glass in an arid wave.

Bunny unhunched his neck and started again for the Olds. Out on the sidewalk I whirled and took down the remaining half of the door. One high and one low. It made a hell of a noise. Anyone coming through that vestibule in a hurry should have thought again about his hurry with a square yard of glass in his hair.

When I turned I caught a flash of the shirt-sleeved man under the clock across the street running into a store. I headed for the car. I nearly yelled out loud when I saw the kid had panicked. All the way to St. Louis we'd gone for a driver, and now he'd panicked. Instead of staying under the wheel and drawing no attention to the car, he'd jumped out and run around and opened the doors on our side. His face was like wet cottage cheese.

Bunny went through the front door in a sliding skid. The kid took one look at my face and started to run back around the front of the Olds. Across the street something went ker-blam!! The kid whinnied like a horse with the colic. He ran in a circle for three seconds and then fell down in front of the Olds, his white cotton gloves in the dirty street and his legs still on the sidewalk. The left side of his head was gone.

Bunny dropped the sack and scrambled for the wheel. I was halfway into the back seat when I heard the car stall out as he tried to give it gas too fast. It was quite a feeling. I backed out again and faced the bank, tried to have eyes in the back of my head for the unseen shotgunner across the street, and listened to Bunny mash down on the starter. The motor caught, finally. I breathed again, but a fat guard galloped out the bank's front doors, his gun hand high over his head. He got it down in a hurry.

I swear both his feet were off the ground when he fired at me. The odds must have been sixty thousand to one, but he took me in the left upper arm. It smashed me back against the car. I steadied myself with a hand on the roof and put two a yard behind each other right through his belt buckle. If they had their windows open they could have heard him across town.

I stumbled into the back seat and Bunny took it out of there. The Olds bumped hard twice as it went over the kid. Across the street I could see the shirt-sleeved man pumping frantically at his jammed shotgun. I raised the Smith & Wesson, and lowered it again. I still needed every bullet. I couldn't afford any luxuries. I got the car doors closed within half a block.

"Handkerchiefs!" I yelled at Bunny as we flew up Central and spun east on Roosevelt on the red. "Ditch those glasses. Slow it down. Stay in traffic." Without looking back he tossed two handkerchiefs over his shoulder, snatched off the dark glasses, and grabbed up a blue beret from the seat beside him. He crammed it down on his yellow head. With the glasses off and his hair hidden he looked like a different person.

I wadded up his handkerchiefs with my own and tried to staunch the double-ended leak in my left arm just below the short sleeve of the sport shirt. I accomplished exactly nothing. All that stuff about a bullet's initial impact being shock with no pain; that's horse manure. I felt it going in and I felt it coming out. Like a red-hot saw-tooth file.

I reloaded the Smith & Wesson. I ignored the warm molasses running down my arm, except to keep it from dripping on my pants. I watched the lights. The kid had had the lights timed all the way back to Yavapai Terrace, but we didn't have the kid. I couldn't sit still. I wanted to get back south of Van Buren again so bad I could taste it.

They had to figure us for a main highway. Highway 80 East, to Tucson and Nogales, if they'd seen the right turn on Roosevelt. North to Prescott or Wickenburg, if they hadn't. Even west, to Yuma and the coast. There'd be road blocks up by now on every main artery out of town. We weren't going out of town. Not yet.

We'd passed Seventh Street while I was fooling with the useless handkerchiefs, Twelfth while I was reloading. The first red light caught us at Sixteenth. We sat in tense silence with people in cars all around us. My guts shriveled down to pebble size. I opened my mouth to holler at Bunny to make a run for it, and closed my teeth down hard. So far we hadn't even heard a siren.

In motion again we sailed up to Twentieth and turned south. We were back across Van Buren before I even had time to begin holding my breath. Past Adams and Washington, over the tracks to East Henshaw, and back toward town at the light. Up to Twelfth in the double-back, a left, and then a right. Shimmering in the sun under a eucalyptus tree, the black Ford sat ahead of us on Yavapai Terrace, close enough to a Chinese grocery to assure that kids wouldn't bother it. Bunny pulled in behind it. We might have been three miles from the bank, but I knew we weren't four.

"Get something out of your bag for this arm," I told Bunny. He was out of the Olds before I had the words all the way out of my mouth, over to the Ford, and back again. He had the jacket to my lightweight suit, and a shirt. "Shred it and fold it and tie it around this thing. Tight." Heat and dust and nausea filled my throat as he complied. I choked it down, whacked some of the dried blood crust from my arm, and slung the jacket loosely over my left shoulder to hide the crude bandage.

After glancing up and down the deserted street, I slid out and followed Bunny back to the Ford. I watched the two-handed carry he made with the sack, and for the first time I wondered how much was in it. In a fifty-pound sack with twenty-five per cent hundreds and the rest twenties, a man can walk away with two hundred thousand dollars. If he walks away.

The Olds we'd leave right here. Bunny pulled ahead to get clear, then backed out onto Twelfth again. He headed south, slowly. The street names were Indian—Papago, Pima, Cocopa, Mohave, Apache—but the area was Mexican. The bushy shade trees were stunted and gnarled. The houses were small, sun-blistered, shacky and close together. The front yards were overgrown tangles. Bunny nosed the Ford into Durango Street, and parked across the street from the dark blue Dodge sedan in the middle of the block.

I drew a long breath as he pulled up the brake. "Okay," I

said. "New script. Listen close. I'm grounded. We're not going to the cabin in the canyon." With the kid gone and me with a torn-up arm we had to throw away the book. I rummaged in the sack at my feet. The first three bundles I picked up were hundreds. Fifteen thousand dollars right in my hand. I dropped two of them back, found two packages of twenties, and shoved the three into a jacket pocket.

"We split up here, big man. You take the Dodge. Duck into a cheap motel. Don't forget to wash the yellow dye out of your hair. Day after tomorrow after dark pull out and head east. Stay off Highways 80 and 66. Go back on 70. Roswell, Plainview . . . that way."

I tried to think of it all. "Take the sack. At Memphis head south for Florida. The gulf coast. Pick a small town. When you make it, once a week mail me a thousand in hundreds, not new bills, registered mail. To Roy Martin, General Delivery, Main Post Office, Phoenix, Arizona. Got it? Take off. I'll join you the minute I can travel."

Bunny got out of the Ford and walked around it and opened the door on my side. His big, hard face was solemn. We shook hands, and he picked up the sack and crossed the drowsy street to the Dodge, his shoes making little puffs in the inch-thick dust. There was a layer of it on the Dodge from passing cars. Bunny opened the back deck, rolled in the sack, and slammed down the lid. With his hand on the door handle he looked over at me and waved before he got in and drove off. Just before he reached the corner I remembered the rest of my clothes were in the Dodge. I reached for the horn, and pulled my hand back. I had more immediate problems than clothes.

I sat there with kind of an all-gone feeling. All the adrenalin-charged-up excitement had drained away. My mind chugged busily, but the rest of me was numb.

Letting the sack go with Bunny hadn't been in the blueprint, but it was the best place for it now. I had some scrambling to do, and the first rule of the game is don't get caught with it on you. If they have to sweet-talk you to try to find out where it is, twenty-to-life has a way of coming out seven-to-ten. If only so they can follow you when you hit the street again. Although on this little frolic, plank-walking the guards could have made everything else academic, if they'd done the big somersault. That one on the sidewalk—

Clean away, except for the hole in my arm. And except for the silly bastard kid. If he'd stayed with the car, I wouldn't be sitting here improvising on an iron-clad plan. Yeah, and if wishes were horses, beggars would ride.

I roused myself, with an effort. I had a lot to do. I had a doctor to find. A doctor would be trouble, but I'd cross that bridge when I came to it. I slid over under the wheel and started up the Ford, and then I had a real bad moment. Bunny's strength pulling up the hand-brake was almost too much for my weakened left arm. Salt perspiration stung my eyes fiercely before I finally succeeded in backing it off. The shirt-bandage was sopping.

Turning the first corner, the sun through the windshield nearly seared my eyeballs. The first two signs I slowed down for in front yards were a realtor and a plumber. The third one drew down the money. Santiago E. Sanfilippo, M.D. I drove by slowly. A garage connected with the house. There was no car in the garage, none in front of the house.

I had no time for anything fancy. I drove up the driveway and into the garage. I draped the jacket over my left shoulder again and walked up the enclosed passageway that led into the house. Through a glass panel in the door I could see an office inside. I had to knock twice before a man in white ducks and a white jacket with a stethoscope sticking out of a pocket opened the door.

Dr. Sanfilippo was a tall, thin, young-looking job, coffee-colored, black-eyed, and good looking. He had a misplaced-eyebrow type of mustache. From the look he gave me I wasn't exactly what he'd been expecting to see. "Yes?" he demanded impatiently when I out-waited him. I couldn't see or hear anyone in the office behind him. "This is a private entrance." He looked over my shoulder at the Ford. "Is that your car? What do you mean by driving it into my garage?"

"I'm a patient, Doc," I told him.

"Then go around to the patients' entrance," he snapped. "And get that automobile out of there before you do."

"Let's arbitrate it, Doc," I showed him the Smith & Wesson about ten inches from his belly. He backed up in a straight line until he ran into a desk behind him. I stepped inside and closed the door. "You alone?"

"I'm alone," he admitted. He looked unhappy about it. "I keep no drugs on the premises," he added. His English was better than mine.

"Inside, Doc." I motioned with the gun and followed him from the cluttered office into a small examination room with whitewashed walls and a wash basin in one corner. Both room and basin looked fairly clean. There was a phone in the office, but none in the examination room. There was only one door, and I was between him and it. A framed diploma hung on the near wall, and I stepped up and read it. It looked legitimate, and I sat down on a white stool beside the elevated examination table. I wanted no self-appointed abortionist whittling on my arm.

Dr. Sanfilippo had been watching me warily. I removed the jacket from my shoulder, and his mustachioed upper lip tightened when he saw the shredded, sodden shirt around my arm. "*Madre de Dios!*" he breathed. His black eyes flicked from a battered radio on a green cabinet back to my arm. "You know I'll have to report this," he said huskily.

"Sure you will," I soothed him. "But you're a doctor. First you'll dress it." I held out the arm. "Like right now."

His smooth, trim features still expressed shock. "Those bank guards—" he began, and stopped. He swallowed, hard. His face was suddenly damp.

"The arm, Doc," I reminded him. So the guards had died. Without ever knowing it, Santiago E. Sanfilippo, M.D., had just passed over an invisible line.

He washed his hands in the basin, and after drying them, unwrapped the arm and examined it, front and back. "Large caliber," he said professionally.

"Large," I agreed.

He turned to the green cabinet. "A half an ampule—"

"No anesthetic," I cut him off.

He shrugged. It was my funeral, and for him it couldn't happen soon enough. He was getting his confidence back. He felt superior to the sweaty, gun-holding type sitting in his office with a ragged bloody hole in his arm. Next he'd be planning my capture. I had a feeling this boy was going to make it easy for me.

He laid out a tray of sharp-looking things on the table, and I spread a towel in my lap. He bathed, swabbed, probed, disinfected, and bandaged. He was rougher than he needed to be. "Don't move until I put a sling on it," he said brusquely when he finished.

"No sling," I said. I picked up the dry end of the towel and mopped off my face. I reached in my jacket pocket where it was slung over my knees, and took out the wrapped package of fifty one-hundred-dollar bills. I broke the seal and put it in my pocket, counted out fifteen bills in three little piles of five each on the examination table, and pushed them toward him. "Nice job, Doc."

That changed his expression *tout de suite*. His tongue ran over his lips, his black eyes never leaving the money. He reached out almost tentatively and picked it up, riffled it nervously, then stuffed it into a wallet and the wallet into his pocket again.

I stood up and kicked the stool I'd been sitting on in his direction. "Sit, Doc. Real still." At the basin where he'd washed up I looked in the small mirror at my short black hair and tanned hard face. I laid the gun on the edge of the basin. I ran the water, and found a clean towel. Stooped over, I could watch his feet. If he could get to me before I got to the gun, he was a better man than I thought. One-handed I washed the oil and lampblack from my hair, and the suntan lotion from my face and neck. When I emerged from behind the towel, Sanfilippo stared in rank disbelief at skin a nationality lighter and iron-gray hair a generation older. "You—you're an old man!" he blurted, incredulously.

"Forty-four, Doc." I patted my crewcut. "The snow on the mountain? Just all the years of taking in washing." His mouth hung open. I looked him over. Thin as he was, I knew I couldn't carry him out of the office. "Walk out to the car ahead of me," I told him. "I'm going to tie you and leave you in the garage."

He didn't like it. He thought it over. I could have predicted the instant he brightened. Would I have paid him if I were going to kill him? Certainly not. The stupid bastard never stopped to realize that if I'd been going to leave him around to do any broadcasting, he'd never have seen me out of the war paint. Following him from the examination room, I picked up something from his surgical tray with a bone handle and six inches of steel. I stuck it in my belt.

In the passageway I got out the Woodsman and put it under my armpit, where I could get to it in a hurry. At the car Sanfilippo turned and looked at me expectantly. I kept a careful ten feet away from him. "Think—something's wrong—" I mumbled, weaving on my feet. I did a long, slow pinwheel to the ground, staying off the bad side. From beneath nearly closed lids I could see Sanfilippo's startled look as he stared down at me. My right hand was close enough to the Woodsman's grip to stop his clock if he came after me, or if he tried to run out of the garage. I didn't expect him to do either. I'd tabbed this guy as a weisenheimer, and I was just egotistical enough to want to make him prove himself out.

He took a final look at me, and spun around to the Ford. He flung open the rear door, and I could hear him pawing through the back seat. He left that in a hurry and tried the front. He ripped out something in Spanish, and darted around to the rear. I'd paid him in hundreds. The swag had to be in the car.

He wasn't bad, the doc. I couldn't see what he used—all I could see were his legs under the Ford—but he popped that back deck lid in no time. I heard the whaaang of broken metal as he snapped the locks on my tool chests in the trunk and went through my stuff like an Indian husking an ear of corn. He sounded off again under his breath, and came around the car on the trot. He dived into the back seat again, only his legs outside.

I eased myself to my feet and got over there. Sanfilippo had a knife out, and was slashing away at the seat cushion. He was right down to the springs in a couple of places. I pulled the surgical tool from my belt. He whacked away at the cushion, cursing like a madman, and then all of a sudden my presence got through to him. He started to turn, and I gave him four and a half inches between the second and third ribs. He was looking over his shoulder at me, and the black eyes didn't believe it. I pulled it out and gave it to him again, then grabbed his belt and steered him down outside the car. He went down like a deflated balloon, slowly at first and then with a rush.

after wiping the handle. I reached down again and yanked his wallet from his hip pocket, stripped it, wiped it, and threw it down beside the body. It would be open and shut to any investigator: killed while pursuing a thief from his office. And, for a bonus, no bullets in him to be matched up with what they took out of the bank guards.

I backed the Ford out of there and drove up to Nineteenth and Van Buren to a big motel, The Tropics. I went in and registered, my jacket again over the bandaged arm. "I'll try your Western hospitality till my office gets me out a new sample line," I told the middle-aged desk clerk. "They busted into my car down in Nogales last night and cleaned me. Clothes, samples, camera—the works. I'll pay you for a week."

The clerk clucked sympathetically as he handed me my change. "Excellent shops within a block or two, sir. Sorry to hear of your misfortune. Hope you enjoy your stay with us."

I took the number 24 key he gave me and ran the car down in front of that unit number. I went inside and locked the door. I washed my face, eased down carefully into an inclined chair with a footrest, and closed my eyes. I had a lot of unwinding to do.

The last conscious thought I had before I drifted off was that those people at the bank were sure going to have one hell of a glass bill.

I lived in that chair for a week, outside of short trips to the on-premises restaurant. Without a sling on the arm I didn't dare get into the big double bed. The first incautious movement would have broken the bullet hole wide open again. With a sling on, I might as well wear a sign "Here I Am." I stayed in the chair.

After the first day I didn't sleep much but I dozed all the time. The next morning I caught a bright-looking busboy in the restaurant, gave him a list of sizes, and sent him out for clothes, specifying long-sleeved sport shirts. He came back with stuff that would have turned a bird of paradise pale with envy. I started to heat up until I happened to think it might be a good switch to have people looking at the clothes instead of at me.

The papers that first morning had a ball. TWO GUARDS SLAIN IN BOLD DAYLIGHT ROBBERY. KILLERS ESCAPE WITH BANK'S $178,000. ONE BANDIT, TWO GUARDS DEAD IN DOWNTOWN SHOOT-EM-UP.

I looked at that figure of $178,000 a couple of times. Even allowing for the bank's president adding in his personal loan account—which isn't exactly unknown—it was still a nice touch.

The newspapers speculated that one of the escapees might have been wounded. The descriptions were interesting, not to say varied. One eye-witness insisted there'd been five of us. The consensus, though, settled for a husky Swede and a little Mexican. Like I said, I'm five ten. I go one seventy, but I've noticed before that a really big man doesn't always seem so big himself. He just makes anyone with him look small.

FBI IN CHARGE, the papers blared. The dear old FBI. I hadn't talked to them in sixteen years, and I wasn't planning to in the next sixteen. They'd trace the kid's prints to St. Louis, and between here and there they'd tear everything up, down, and sideways. And a hell of a lot of good it would do them; when he left St. Louis, the kid didn't know where he was going, and either Bunny or I was with him all the time to make sure he didn't talk about who he was going with. It should make for less heat on the west coast of Florida.

Way on an inside page there was a short paragraph. Area Physician Stabbed In Garage, the small-type headline said. The story continued: The body of Santiago E. Sanfilippo, M.D., 31, of—. I read it three times before I put the paper down. The police would be out rounding up all known arm blasters and goofball users. It plugged the last hole the kid had kicked in the blueprint by not staying with the car.

I wasn't afraid of Bunny's getting picked up. He had the best natural protective coloration I'd ever seen. It was one of the reasons I'd picked him, that and his nerve and his confidence in me. I've been in this business a while. Two guys with guts and a go-to-hell-with-you-Jack regard for consequences have about three chances in ten of pulling off a big, well-planned smash-and-grab. If one of them can shoot like me and the other one is Bunny, the odds are a damn sight better.

The first week I had a fever nearly all the time. The arm needed treatment, but I couldn't get treatment. I swallowed aspirin by the gross. When the thing wasn't throbbing it was itching. I let it throb and I let it itch. The second week my temperature was gone, but my legs felt like two pieces of spaghetti. I'd wake from a nap dripping with sweat, and have to change from the skin out.

It was lonely in that motel room. Around the country when I hide out I always have a dog and usually a couple of cats with me. Animals I like. People I can do without.

For the first five days the headlines had us as having been sighted in half the towns between Guantanamo, Cuba, and Nome, Alaska. After that we dropped back onto the ninth page, and then right on out of the news. The third week I began to take an interest in a menu again, instead of just shoveling something down. The arm was going to be all right. A couple of times when it had been real bad I'd debated slipping down into Nogales and trying for a doctor. I decided I couldn't risk it. If they didn't watch anyplace else in the world, they'd watch that Mexican border.

About the middle of the third week I drove uptown to the main post office. From its front steps I could have thrown a stone kitty-cornered across the street to the bank we'd taken. I could see they had new glass doors up.

I had a wallet full of crap identifying the non-existent Roy Martin. There were two envelopes at the window, and I signed for them. In the car I slit the first one and unwrapped ten hundred-dollar bills neatly sealed in oilskinned paper. The second was a duplicate. There was no message in either. The return address said Dick Pierce, General Delivery, Hudson, Florida. Bunny had made it big.

Five days later there was another envelope.

Seven days later there wasn't.

The mail clerk handed me a telegram addressed to Roy Martin. I got away from him fast and opened it. IN TROUBLE STAY PUT DO NOTHING WILL CALL YOU. DICK.

I stared blankly at the recruiting posters on the post office walls. Bunny was in trouble, all right, but not the kind I

15

was supposed to think. The telegram was a clinker. When we'd first teamed up, I'd arranged with Bunny that a message from either of us calling for a change in plans had to be signed "Abie."

But that was nothing compared to the other thing the matter with the telegram. If he lived to be a hundred and four, Bunny would never call me about anything. The knife slash that had left him with the livid throat scar had reached his vocal cords. Bunny was a mute.

Bunny hadn't sent the telegram.

The only person who could have was someone who had intercepted a thousand-dollar envelope for Roy Martin. I looked at the telegram again. It had originated in Hudson, Florida.

I drove back to The Tropics and found Hudson on an atlas. It was a crossroads town south of Perry on U.S. 19 on the way down to Tampa.

I checked out.

The soreness was gone from the shoulder, but it was still stiff. It would have to do. Three-fifty, four hundred miles a day, I figured, without killing myself. Five days.

Knowing Bunny, I was sure of the only way he could have been dealt out of the game.

I had business in Hudson, Florida.

I settled down behind the wheel.

The only time I was ever in the pen, the boss headshrinker gave me up as a bad job. "You're amoral," the prison psychiatrist told me. "You have no respect for authority. Your values are not civilized values." That was after he'd flipped his psychiatric lid at his inability to pierce my defense mechanism, as he called it. I had him taped from the first sixty seconds. He didn't care what I was; he just wanted to know how I got that way. It was none of his damn business. I gave him nothing but a hard way to go.

Oh, I could have told him things. I could have told him about the kitten. I was maybe eleven or twelve. Fifth or sixth grade. I saw this kitten in the window of a pet shop. A blue Persian, although right then I couldn't have told the difference from a spotted Manx. I ran my finger across the glass and watched her little pink nose and big bronze eyes follow it, and I knew she was for me.

I went back to the house to make my case. I wasn't from any underprivileged home. The kitten's price might have jolted them, but I wasn't in the habit of asking for much. I was the youngest in the family and I had a bushel of sisters and aunts. Getting me the kitten became a family project. The family had also had for some time a project to get me to play more with the neighborhood kids. I'd given up trying to explain to them that the other kids gave me a pain, king-sized.

The sisters and aunts did a lot of yatating before I got the kitten. They always did a lot of yatating. Once—I was fifteen, maybe—eight or nine of them were going it forty to the dozen in the living room. I stuck my head in the door and gave them my very best rebel yell. When they climbed down off the tables and chairs, I told them: "The male of the species gives voice." They didn't think it was funny.

But that was later.

I named the kitten Fatima. First syllable accented, all short vowel sounds. It seemed to suit her coppery eyes and smoky coloring. I played with her by the hour. I taught her tricks. No one teaches a kitten anything it doesn't want to learn, but Fatima humored me. We had a wonderful time together.

I still got a load of guff frequently from the family about not participating more with my age group. That's probably not the way they put it then; it's not the day before yesterday I'm talking about. I paid no attention to them. I had Fatima, and she was all the company I needed. In some moods she was a natural-born clown, but in others she had an aloof dignity. I'd never have believed that anything so tiny could be so fearless. Fatima would have tackled a lion if one had got in her way.

Some organization in the town gave a pet show. YWCA, Junior League, Woman's Club, American Legion Auxiliary, B.P.O.E. Does—I don't remember which, but I remember women were running it. I bought a little red leash for

Fatima out of my paper route money, and entered her in the show. I liked having a paper route. It was something I could do myself, not some group project I was always being pushed to get into with a bunch of moronic kids.

Fatima and her red leash knocked their eyes out at the pet show. She was a real ham. She sat up in the center of the outdoor ring and went through her whole bag of tricks, better than she'd do them for me in private. She went through the kitten and cat classes like a streak of blue lightning, and we were brought back for best-in-show. In the ring for the final judging there was Fatima, a big boxer dog, a black rabbit, a hamster, a goat, and a bowl of tropical fish shaded from the sunlight.

The boxer belonged to a kid who went to the same school I did, a fat tub of lard a grade or so ahead of me. I knew him by sight. If I ever knew his name, I'd forgotten it. When I saw the boxer, I steered Fatima around to the other side of the ring. She just plain didn't like dogs. The fat boy saw what I was doing, and he followed me in a smart-alecky way. Fatima swelled her throat ruff and hissed at the boxer in a Persian's surprisingly loud hiss. The fat boy laughed. I asked him to move his dog away. Deliberately he gave him more leash. The boxer leaned down for a closer look, and quicker than I can say it, Fatima raked his nose. The boxer snarled, and snapped. Just once.

Fatima lay in the grass, one tiny little dot of blood on her ruff. Her neck had been broken. The big dog nosed at the inanimate bit of blue-gray fur, then looked up at me as though half-ashamed. I didn't blame the boxer. He'd done the natural thing for any dog. I picked up Fatima's body, and turned blindly away. All I wanted was to get out of there. The fat boy—who first looked scared, and then defiant—grabbed my arm and spun me around. "Look!" he crowed. "Look it him! Cryin' like a baby!"

I beat the stuffing out of him.

The women got me off him, finally. I was scuffed up and so were they. There was a hell of a lot of gabble-gabble. I walked out on it. I took Fatima home and buried her in the back yard.

That was Saturday. Sunday I hung around the house most of the day. Monday afternoon I waited in the schoolyard for the fat boy to come out, and I beat the stuffing out of him all over again.

That night his father came over to my house. There was a big pow-wow. My family was surprised to learn about Fatima's having been killed. They hadn't even missed her. Finally they settled everything to their satisfaction. The fat boy's father would get me another kitten, and I would apologize to the fat boy.

I told them no. I was nice and polite, but I told them no. When they jumped me for reasons, I told them I didn't want anything from anyone. My father took me upstairs for a talk. I listened, and said nothing. When he saw he was getting nowhere, he went back downstairs. The meeting broke up with them all making baffled noises at each other.

The next afternoon at school I had to chase the fat boy from the schoolyard clear over to within a couple blocks from his house before I caught him. It didn't help him when I did.

There was a lot of telephoning around that night. My father was mad. He took me upstairs again and gave me a licking. He said we were going over to the fat boy's house, and I was going to apologize. I was still crying from the licking, but I told him I wouldn't say it after he got me over there. He made a lot of spluttering sounds and walked out of the bedroom. We didn't go anywhere.

Later that night the minister came to our house. He talked to me for a long time. All about the unexplainable things that happen in life, and the necessity for understanding. I understood, all right. What was all the talk about? I understood. I listened to him, though. I was polite. I wasn't going to give them a chance to call me surly or bad-mannered. When he was tired talking, the minister went away. I don't think even he thought he'd accomplished much.

The fat boy wasn't in school the next day. I was disappointed. When I got home there was something for me. The fat boy's father had left a carrying case with a blue Persian kitten. I didn't say anything to my mother or my sisters. I took the case out in the back yard, and when they stopped watching to see what I was doing I walked crosslots downtown to the pet shop and gave the case and the kitten back to the pet shop man. I told him to give the fat boy's father his money back. The pet shop man looked funny, but he took the kitten. He didn't say a word.

When he got home that night my father blew his stack. I didn't answer him back when he started in on me. All I wanted was to be left alone, and no one would leave me alone. My father said I was damn well going to do what I was told to do, and that if the kitten wasn't back in the house by the next night the consequences would be mine. I knew it just wasn't going to be that way.

So when I got a licking the next night it was partly for having caught the fat boy again on his way home from school, and partly for not having gone back to the pet shop for the kitten.

The next day in school I was called down to the principal's office. He talked a long time, too. The gist of it was that one more go-round with the fat boy and I would be expelled from school. I asked him politely what it had to do with school. I can still see his face tightening up, muscle by muscle. He said sharply that I was persevering in an attitude I would regret to the last day I lived but he never did answer my question.

The fat boy wasn't in school that day, but I got a licking anyway that night for not having brought the kitten home. I got another the next night, and another the next. By then they were ritualistic, without a word being said on either side. I overheard my mother arguing with my father about his handling of me. I was sorry to hear it. I didn't want sympathy. I didn't want anything. I was stronger than they were, and I knew it. I had undivided purpose. I didn't feel like a martyr. I felt like someone doing what he had to do.

At school I was having trouble finding the fat boy. He was leaving by different doors, at different times. It was three more days before I caught him again. The next morning I was back in the principal's office. He wasn't there, but his secretary told me I was expelled. She looked kind of funny at me all the time she was telling me. I just kind of hung around during the day and went home at the usual time.

My mother and sisters were all waiting for me. At first I thought it was about being expelled, but they hadn't heard. They'd bought me a different Persian kitten. I thanked them. I wasn't mad at them about anything. I wasn't mad at my father about anything. Because the new kitten was a poor dumb animal that needed my help, I fed it. I didn't play with it.

My father came home early, in a tearing rage. The principal had called him. When he saw the new kitten and learned where it had come from, he clouded up and thundered at the women about going behind his back. They turned on him *en masse*. It astonished him. They didn't back him up, exactly, but for the first time in better than a week I got to bed that night without a licking. Even to myself I had to admit I was glad of it. My right shoulder had been hurting worse each of the past three days. I made a bed for the new kitten, and went to bed early myself.

By noon the next day I had caught up on lickings. Before breakfast I slipped out of the house and waited for the fat boy on his way to school. By now he screamed just like a girl at the sight of me. I was in the house at ten thirty when my father came home and marched me upstairs. He really laid it into me. These days they might send a twelve year old to a home, or to reform school. Then they didn't. My father didn't know anything to do but lick me. About an hour afterward I was sick to my stomach.

I didn't go downstairs for lunch. My stomach still felt bad and my shoulder was really giving me a hard time. I tried lying down, but that made the shoulder worse. Around two o'clock my mother came into my room. She looked at my eyes, put her hand on my forehead, and called the doctor. When he came he said I had a broken collarbone. He strapped me up like a mummy. He asked a lot of questions about the marks on me. I didn't answer him. It was none of his business. Afterward I could hear him talking to my mother out in the hall.

I took it easy that afternoon. Mostly I wondered how I was going to keep after the fat boy with an arm strapped down. I knew I'd find a way. As it turned out, I didn't need to. I was sitting downstairs leafing through an encyclopedia when my next oldest sister came flying into the house. She ran past into the kitchen without seeing me, and I could hear her breathlessly telling my mother that there was a big moving van in front of the fat boy's house.

The fat boy's family was moving away.

I don't know why I was so sure they were moving out of town. Maybe because I knew they were sure I'd find him if it was anywhere in the same town. I sat there looking at a picture of a Roman legion in full battle-dress, and I felt a deep sense of peace.

And just like that, it ended.

The shoulder healed in five weeks. In eight they let me back into school. Around the house the subject was never mentioned.

In a year I think everyone had honestly forgotten.

Except me.

I made El Paso the first night.

Highway 70 through Mesa, Safford, and Duncan in Arizona brought me into Lordsburg, New Mexico. Between Safford and Duncan the desert is for real. The stark, multicolored rock and sand of buttes and coulees grimly overshadow the sparse greenery of saguaro, mesquite, and palos verde.

Highways 70 and 80 join up at Lordsburg and run together through Deming to Las Cruces. I turned south there on 80 to El Paso. The temperature when I left Phoenix had been eighty-five. Rolling past the railroad marshaling yards in El Paso there was a flurry of snow in the headlights. Altitude makes a difference. The speedometer on the Ford said 409 miles when I pulled into a motel on the east side of town.

I'd pushed it a bit to make El Paso. I had a reason. I had to get my arm attended to before the bandage became a part of the tissue. Across the International Bridge in Juarez I knew where I could get it attended to, and no questions asked.

The motel office had signs on the desk advertising fabulous guided tours of the fabulous city of Ciudad Juarez in fabulous Old Mexico. I had them call their agency, and in thirty minutes a pot-bellied little Mex in a business suit showed up to guide me. He was about thirty-five, and had the eyes of a well-fed weasel. Four dollars changed hands, and we took off in his car.

He was a cheerful talker. Compulsive, rather. He had been baptized Jaime Carlos Torreon Garcia, he told me, but his friends called him Jimmy. He worked for Pan Am in El Paso, but lived in Juarez. He guided nights and weekends. Would I care to see the most excellent Mexican filigreed silver, handworked? I regretted that on Mexican filigreed handworked silver I was loaded. Jimmy was too old a hand at the game even to look disappointed.

It was a twenty minute ride from the motel to the bridge. On the way across Jimmy had a sparkling salute for everyone at the check-in stations, English for the U.S. guards, Spanish for the Mexican soldiers. Unanimously profane in their replies to him, none of them bothered to look at me. The number of trips he made over that bridge, he was better known than the president of the country. Either country.

The fabulous city of Ciudad Juarez was—as always—dirty, dusty, and squalid. Except when it rained, and then it was muddy beyond belief. Mexican authorities show a reluctance to put drains in their streets. God sends the rain and the mud. God will take it away.

My mentor headed unerringly for a bar. "My friend," he told me, with an encompassing wave of his hand at the swarthy, shock-headed proprietor. "He has the finest *cantina* in the old town."

I looked around at the empty booths and fly-specked walls. "He's not a relative?" I asked Jimmy.

"My cousin," he admitted blandly. Since I so obviously knew the rules of the road, he sat down and ordered Canadian Club for us both without consulting my taste.

"Have a couple," I told him. "Take your time. I'm going to walk around to the Street of the Girls."

He slid from his stool immediately. "I must go with you," he protested. "They will cheat you, amigo."

"I'm the bashful type, Jaime Carlos," I said. "I'll go it alone. I'll pay you your commission just as you'd get it from the house." He eyed me doubtfully but returned to his Canadian Club.

Out on the street I side-doored it a couple of times to make sure he wasn't following me. I couldn't see any sign of him, although probably at least half the Mexican male population resembled him in outline. I turned up the third street on the left. I hadn't been in Juarez in years, but I knew where I wanted to go. The side street macadam ended ten yards in from the intersection, and the sidewalk vanished and dropped down eight inches to an earthen footpath.

I found the old woman's place with no trouble at all. I recognized the half-rusted-away iron fence around the scurfy, postage-stamp-sized front yard the minute I saw it. The last time I'd been here Ed Morris had been with me. Ed had been pushing up daisies quite a while now.

The old woman looked me over through a hole in the door panel when I knocked. I don't know what she thought she saw, but she unbolted the door. There was no conversation. She tested the bill I gave her under three different lights while I took off my shirt. Her fat hand made a swooping movement somewhere into her clothes, and emerged without the bill.

She went to work on the arm, humming to herself in a tuneless monotone. I'd been afraid she might have to steam the old bandage free, but she cut it carefully in several places and with little dabs of ether worked it loose. She knew her business. It wasn't a painless operation but considering the length of time it had gone unattended it went a damn sight easier than I'd expected.

I looked at the scar while she prepared a new bandage. A beauty contest queen might have hollered foul, but it was healing. The new bandage was smaller and more compact, easier to hide. The old woman never opened her mouth while she put it on. The last time I'd been there she'd looked three years older than the Archangel Michael, and she sure as hell hadn't found the Fountain of Youth in the meantime.

Outside again I headed back up to the corner. As I stepped back up on the sidewalk, I turned automatically for a look behind me. A street light away I could see a figure of Jimmy's general dimensions. It bothered me. I stepped into a doorway and gave the half-seen figure a chance to catch up. I waited five minutes, but nobody passed my doorway. I wasn't satisfied, but I had to be satisfied. I used my handkerchief to wipe the red dust of the earthen footpath from my shoes, and walked back to the cantina.

Jaime Carlos Torreon Garcia wasn't there.

His cousin, the bushy-haired proprietor, looked surprised to see me. "No sport?" he inquired with a raised eyebrow.

"No sportsman," I said. "Too old."

"It comes to all of us," he philosophized, but crossed himself against the approach of the evil day.

Jimmy bustled in the front door. He, too, seemed surprised to see me. His well-managed expressions of first astonishment and then sympathy would have gone down better with me if it hadn't been for the thick coating of red dust on his shoes.

The second I saw it I was in motion. I tossed a bill down on the bar and hustled him out of there before he could speak. Whatever he knew, it was going to stay with him. Let the cousin think my sudden exit the frustrated petulance of a sexual loser. Cousin Jimmy had acquired some dangerous knowledge.

I sat in Jimmy's car and thought it over. Beside me he kept shooting nervous little glances at me. If he had information, I was sure he wouldn't know what to do with it. He needed to put his head together with someone and plan a financial coup based on his knowledge of the gringo's movements. Jaime Carlos Torreon Garcia had the proper piratical instincts but a deficiency in a method of operation. And he wasn't going to live long enough to acquire one.

"I think I've had enough sightseeing," I told him, turning toward him. Under cover of the movement I got the Woodsman into my hand. "I think you have, too." I showed him the gun. His eyes popped like a frog's on a hot rock. "Drive up to the checkout zone. Tell them 'no purchases' in Spanish. Just that. Nothing more. Let's hear you say it."

"*No compra*," he said huskily.

"That's *all* you'll say," I warned him. "Let's go."

At the barrier he had trouble getting that much out, let alone anything else. We went through in a breeze. I repeated my warning before we reached the U.S. inspection station. Two minutes later we were back across the bridge. I felt better. Trouble in Mexico I didn't want. Authorities there have a habit of tossing a gringo into a flea-infested calaboose and conveniently losing the key. Sometimes a man can buy his way out. Sometimes he can't.

That left Jimmy.

"Drive up one of these side streets," I told him.

He nearly let go of the wheel. "S-señor, don't do this theeng, I beg of you! Don't do—"

"Left, Jimmy. Now." The car lurched around as he yanked convulsively at the wheel. In three hundred yards the street lights spaced out conveniently. We were about half a mile from the motel, comfortable walking distance. "Pull over. Park between the lights." He did so, babbling unintelligibly in a half-English, half-Spanish high-pitched wail. I rapped him on the arm to snap him out of it. "Dump out your pockets on the seat. Be quick."

It was dark, but I could see. About the third item he showered down on the seat cushion was a pocket knife of the type known as Nacional. Heavy-bladed, in a solid casing, it's a lethal weapon. Jimmy was still turning out his pockets. I picked up the knife and opened it.

I don't know if he saw the movement of my arm or heard the flick of the opening blade. He screamed hoarsely and went for the door handle. I grabbed his collar and jerked him back. He collapsed beside me like a blob of melted butter, his high, keening voice yammering at me. I hit him in the belly to shut him up.

In the sudden silence I took his neck in my hand and found the carotid artery with my thumb. I opened the door on my side. A carotid can be messy. I didn't want to get splashed. I braced my heels against the floorboard and reached for him.

And hesitated.

In the quiet I seemed able to think for the first time since I'd seen clinging red dust on this man's shoes. I'd let myself get so upset at my stupidity in letting the fool follow me that I hadn't thought the thing through.

Alive, he'd talk. Later, if not sooner. That I knew.

But dead, his body would talk, and even more to the point. His cousin expected him back with a tale of where he had followed the *turista*. If he didn't come back, the cousin might get nervous. If he went to the police, they'd have little trouble tracing Jaime Carlos to the motel through the agency. I had had the motel call the agency. The motel would furnish the police with a description of me. And of the Ford.

Dead, this man was an anchor around my neck.

Alive? Not much better, but a little better.

I clicked the knife blade shut. "Sit up and listen to me," I said to him.

He gave a kind of shuddering sigh. "S-señor, I *implore*—"

"Shut up. Drive back to the motel."

It took him a full minute to get the car started. His coordination was gone. He drove like a sleepwalker. In the street lights his face looked like wax. The car bounced high as he turned into the motel driveway going too fast. For a second I thought we were going to take out a cabin before he hit the brake and we skidded in the gravel.

I got out, and motioned at him. "Take off, man."

He stared out at me suspiciously. Was it a trick? It didn't take him long to decide if it was—he still liked it better than where he'd been. He tramped on the accelerator. His car hit the street doing forty-five.

He'd been right up to the gates, and he knew it. He might not know why, but he knew it. As a type he should head straight for his bed and stay there with the covers over his head for three days.

But I couldn't count on it.

Five minutes after his tail-lights winked out of the motel driveway, I was headed east in the Ford.

It was odd in a way about the fat boy's family leaving town that time. Six years later it was my family who were going to leave.

The way it happened was like getting struck by lightning. I was eighteen, in my senior year in high school. It was late in the spring, and after a succession of chilly, rainy days we'd finally caught a hot one. I had my sweater over my arm when I came out the school's back entrance and cut through the parking lot like I did every day on my way home. I saw these four policemen standing in the middle of the lot, and I wondered what they were doing there.

I knew one of them, Harry Coombs, and I nodded as I

passed. He said something to the others and the biggest one, who had been standing with his back to me, turned around to look. "You," he said to me. "Come over here."

I went over to them. I knew who the big one was without really knowing him. His name was Edwards, and he was a sergeant. He was a beefy man with thinning red hair. I didn't like him. No good reason. His voice was too loud. He took up too much of the sidewalk when he swaggered by. Things like that.

He looked me up and down when I stood in front of them. "What d'you know about hubcaps missing from the faculty cars three times a week?" he demanded. He looked hot and uncomfortable, still in his winter uniform.

"I don't know anything about it," I answered him. I didn't, except what I'd been hearing in school assemblies for a month.

The lower lip in his red face swelled pugnaciously. "Harry here says you spend enough time in this parking lot to be able to tell us what's going on," he continued aggressively.

"I said I see him going through here on his way home!" Coombs cut in.

Edwards paid him no attention. "Well?" he said to me.

"You think whoever's doing it waits for me to come by so I can see them?" I was mad. "Or maybe you think I'm doing it?"

"I'll ask the questions," he snapped, scowling. "What's your name?" I told him. I was liking him less and less by the second. "Now you know you must've seen what's been going on out here. Who you covering up for?"

I looked at Harry Coombs, to see if Edwards was kidding. Harry looked away. "Look, you can't mean it," I said finally. "I don't—"

"Answer the question!" Edwards roared at me.

I turned and started to walk away. He grabbed me by the arm. I've always hated having people put their hands on me. I jerked my arm out of his hand. He must have outweighed me three to one, but I caught him on the wrong foot. He staggered sideways two or three paces. His red face looked bloated.

My sweater fell off my arm, and I stooped automatically

to pick it up. Edwards kicked me, hard. I went over and down, flat, skinning my palms on the parking lot cinders.

I scrambled up and went after him, the hate of the world in my heart. Before I could reach him Harry Coombs had me clamped in a bear hug. He was muttering in my ear but I was struggling so hard I didn't hear him. I had my head twisted around yelling at him to let me go. I never even saw Edwards when he stepped up and slapped me heavily in the face.

"Goddammit, sarge!" Coombs said angrily. His arms relaxed, then tightened as I lunged.

"Shut up, you!" Edwards barked at him. "This is a wise one. We'll take him down to the station and talk to him."

"Then take him down yourself," Coombs said. Deliberately he released me. "I'm on duty right here."

"You're on duty where I tell you you're on duty, Coombs," Edwards warned him. "Get him in the patrol car, and get in yourself." The sergeant clumped heavily back to the other two who had been silently standing by.

It was only by an effort of will I kept a hand away from my smarting face. Don't fight it, I told myself. Not here. I walked toward the cruiser parked in a corner of the lot. Harry Coombs tramped along beside me, muttering under his breath.

The five of us rode downtown. I never said a word. In the police station one of the ones who had taken no part previously took me by the arm and led me to a door beyond which were two steel cells with cement floors. He motioned me inside. I went in and looked around. There was a steel cot without even a blanket on it. Nothing else. The policeman didn't close the cell door, but he closed the outside door. I got a good look at his face before he went out.

I sat down on the cot and tried to get myself organized. I knew they'd be coming in. I didn't feel worried, just mad. I knew I was going to get that Edwards some day if it was the last thing I ever did. And if it could be today, so much the better.

I stood up quickly when the outside door opened. It was only Harry Coombs. He closed it and stood with his back to it. "Listen, kid," he said to me hurriedly. "I got through to him at last that you're no juvenile delinquent. He don't think so much of himself right now, but when he comes in here he'll make a little noise to justify himself. Get smart. Do what he says, y'hear?" I looked at him. "Ahhhh, you're as thick as he is," Coombs growled, and walked out.

I took off my shoes and put them on the steel cot beside me, and stretched out on my back. I stared up at the ceiling covered with misty cracks. Do what Edwards told me? Not a chance. Not a bloody chance. If he was on a hook because of me, he'd stay there till his liver and lungs rotted for all the help he'd get from me.

I sat up when the outer door opened again. Three of them filed in, Edwards in the lead. I didn't know the names of the other two, but by now I knew their faces. Harry Coombs wasn't with them. I sat there and watched them come in.

"Let's hear the answers to a few questions, now," Edwards began. His voice was rough. He looked the same, his red face shiny, but even without what Coombs had said I knew he didn't sound the same. His voice said he didn't like where he was. "I want a statement from you as to what you were doing in that parking lot," he blustered. "A signed, witnessed statement."

I didn't say anything. His face grew dark. He walked toward me, slowly. I sat still. "I said I want a statement from you!" he bellowed.

I sat there. Any statement I gave him he could probably twist around for his own purposes. He'd get no statement from me. When I said nothing, Edwards made a slight movement with his left hand. Just a gesture. Testing my nerve. I sat there. "God, how I love you boy scout tough guys!" he said between his teeth. He loomed up over me as I sat on the cot. He jabbed me in the ribs with a stiffened thumb. "Stand up when I talk to you!"

I sat there. He slapped me. My head hit the wall behind me. One of the men with him made some sort of sound, whether assent or protest I don't know. I couldn't see them. All I could see was Edwards' bulk, his red face and his hot-looking little eyes. My own were squeezed hard trying to keep the tears behind them. "Stand up, damn you!" Edwards barked. He stiffened the thumb and advanced it slowly toward my ribs, waiting for me to flinch. I didn't flinch. He jabbed me in the ribs. He jabbed me again. And again. Each time it felt like a red-hot poker.

When I saw he meant to keep it up, I reached around in back of me and picked up one of my shoes by the toe. When Sergeant Edwards' arm moved again, I came up out of there, fast. I smashed him right across the bridge of the nose with the heel of the shoe. I hit him with every ounce I had in me. He went reeling backward, blood spurting like a gusher. Only the men behind him kept him from going down. He rebounded from them and clubbed at me with both fists. He hit me about three more shots on my way down to the floor. On my way up I hit him in the belly with both hands. He knocked me down again.

There was a lot of noise and confusion. People yelling. People hurting me. I couldn't see very well. I went down and got up twice more. I think it was twice. If I could have seen Edwards, I'd have butted him squarely in the middle of his ugly face with the top of my skull.

But I couldn't see him.

And after a while I couldn't get up any more.

It seemed like a long time later I heard my father's voice. I wondered how he'd got there. "—Someone's going to sweat for this," he was saying angrily. "And I don't care if it's you, John!"

I opened my eyes cautiously. I could see from the left one. I was in an iron bed, and my father and John Mullen, the Chief of Police, were nose to nose at its foot.

"Take it easy, Karl," the chief said. John Mullen lived just up the street from us. I'd taken his youngest daughter, Kathy, to one of the school dances. "I'll get to the bottom of it."

"You're damn right you will!" my father said hotly. "And I want him moved out of here to a hospital right this minute!"

"Doc Everhardt says it isn't necessary, Karl."

"Don't try to tell me what's not necessary! I said right now! Don't think you can keep my boy from the treatment he needs just because you've got a stinking situation you'd like to cover—"

"I said I'd get to the bottom of it!" Flint-edged steel

ridged Chief Mullen's tone. His voice had risen, too. "The boy could have been at fault, too, Karl."

"Fault? Fault? Good God, John, have you gone out of your mind? If he burned down the orphans' home, should he look like this? I know this Edwards. A thug in a uniform. A disgrace—"

Chief Mullen had seen my opened eye. He walked quickly around the end of the bed. "What happened, son?" he asked quietly. My father pushed in beside him where he stood looking down at me.

I had to make three starts before I could get out anything. "I—fell down," I said finally. My voice was a breathy rasp.

"Fell!" my father echoed incredulously. "Fell?" He stared at me, then whirled on the chief. "What kind of intimidation is this, John? I'm going—"

"Take it easy, Karl." There was a warning note in the official voice. The chief's shrewd eyes were studying me. "Don't forget we walked in here together. Don't let me hear you say 'intimidation' again." He was still looking down at me thoughtfully. "We'll talk to him later."

"We'll talk to him right now, damn it!"

But the chief finally got my father out of there.

I never told them any more than that, then or later. I never knew what Edwards told them. I didn't care. I think my father thought at first the beating had affected my mind. Right from the beginning, the chief came closer to the truth. Day after day he came to the house with patient questions. After a while I stopped answering him at all. Eventually he stopped coming.

I was out of school three weeks until my face healed up. When I went back, I still had three broken fingers on my left hand, and from shoulders to knees I was spotted like a leopard. I didn't remember anything about the fingers. They must have got stepped on.

Nobody at school—or anywhere else—knew what happened. The police didn't say anything and I didn't say anything. I found out without too much trouble that the two men in the cell with Edwards that day had been Glenn Smith and Walt Cummings.

I took to skipping classes at school, even whole days. I spent more time out of the house at night than I ever had.

The first three marking periods I'd been on the honor roll, and the school office called me in about my sliding grades. They said I might not even graduate if I didn't straighten up. I didn't give a damn. With such a short way to go I didn't think they could flunk me after the marks I'd carried, but I didn't care if they did. I was busy.

Glenn Smith was easy. He was a heavy drinker. I watched him till I found out he spent a lot of time in the Parokeet Tavern. He had a habit of parking his car on the street in back, and walking up a narrow alley to the Parokeet's back door. Sometimes he was in uniform.

Late one night he came back down the alley, staggering a little. I formed a one-man reception committee. I took him from behind, and I lumped him good. I kicked in a few of his ribs, finally, and left him crawling around on the ground like a wingless beetle. He never even got a look at me. I felt good all the way home.

The next morning Chief Mullen came over to school and took me out of my history class. We went outside and sat in his car. He talked for a long time. He didn't accuse me of anything. I knew he couldn't, because Glenn Smith had never seen me.

The chief went on about the idiocy of people attempting to take the law into their own hands. He talked like a damn fool. I'd taken the law into my own hands, and I liked the feel of it. The chief must have seen the expression on my face. He stopped talking and opened his car door. I went back into school.

Walt Cummings took longer. It was better than a month before I found out he dropped in a couple of nights a week at a married woman's a mile out of town. When I had him clocked so I could depend on him, I caught him at her back door one night. I smothered him in wet-down potato sacking as he came out. I got him down, and when I finished with him they carried him in from there. I went home and went to bed.

Chief Mullen was at our house before breakfast the next morning. He was really warm under the collar. He asked me point blank what I knew about Cummings. My father saved me the trouble of lying. He jumped in and wanted to know if the chief was accusing me of anything. Either make a charge you can support, he told Mullen when the chief hesitated, or get out of my house. The chief left, red in the face. I almost laughed out loud. My father didn't ask me anything afterward. He didn't seem comfortable with me.

Two down and one to go. Every time I passed Sergeant Edwards on the street, I smiled at him. Every time I smiled, he scowled. He knew. I wanted him to know. His scowls said plainly he wasn't letting his nerves get jumped up by any crackpot kid. He watched himself, though. He watched himself so well I couldn't get anywhere near him.

School let out. I graduated, barely. My college entrance credits were all shot. I'd have to pass exams to get in. I didn't take the exams. I hung around all summer, into the fall. Twice my father, exasperated, demanded that I get a job if I had no intention of continuing with my schooling. I paid no attention. I had a job. A job I had to take care of before I could look for a job.

Harry Coombs cornered me late one Saturday night when I was coming out of a diner on his beat. He herded me into a corner. "I suppose I'm lucky they sent me out of there before they went into the cell with you that day?" he inquired, prodding me in the chest with his nightstick. I grinned at him. "They're going to sit you down in a square-looking chair one of these days, kid," he told me. "They'll turn on the juice, and there'll be a sizzling noise while they burn your ass up, but you won't hear it. Think it over." He walked away from me.

By October I knew more about Sergeant Edwards than his wife did, but he never gave me an opening. I began to get restless. I didn't know what I was going to do after I got through with him, but I wanted to get it over with and find out.

Then early in November we had an unexpected sleet-and-ice storm. Edwards came up his porch steps that night with his chin shrunk down into his coat collar, careful of the slippery footing. His head was lowered against the stinging blasts. He never saw the piece of pipe I got him with before he reached his front door. When I finished with the pipe, I rolled him back down his porch steps, and went home. He was lucky. Someone found him before he froze to death.

I didn't find that out until morning. Or at least the clock

said it was morning but it was still dark outside. A police cruiser came by for my father and me. They hardly gave us time to dress. My father kept asking them what had happened. They wouldn't say anything. In the cruiser my father kept sneaking looks at me from the corner of his eye.

At the station Chief Mullen really gave me a going-over. He was trying to scare answers out of me. He should have known better by that time. For twenty solid minutes I sat there and smiled at him. I never said a word. My father horned in finally and asked Mullen what basis he had for his unfounded accusations. It really flipped the chief. You've got a wild animal running loose around town, he told my father. You've got a choice. Cage him, or leave town. Leave town, he repeated with emphasis. Better all around.

I felt like laughing until I saw the stricken look on my father's face. I couldn't understand it. The chief couldn't do anything. Nobody could do anything. I didn't give a damn what they thought they knew about me. They couldn't prove a thing.

On the way home my father said tiredly he hoped I'd realize some day it was necessary to live with people. He said a lot of other things. I felt sorry for him. He just couldn't stand up to a situation.

I couldn't believe it when the FOR SALE sign went up on our front lawn. I was disgusted. My father was letting them bluff him right out of the game. They couldn't make him do a thing he didn't agree to do. That's why I couldn't understand it. My father was a weakling.

I couldn't let his spinelessness affect my mother and sisters. I left home that night. I knew I could manage. Obviously my father couldn't.

I left.

I never went back.

I had to switch cars.

The minute my pot-bellied Mexican guide's tongue came unlatched, the police would get a description of the Ford—and of me—from the motel. It didn't matter a damn they wouldn't know why they were looking for me. It was up to me to change the appearance of what they'd be looking for.

Highway 80 east out of El Paso is a long, straight, black stretch of road. Not many headlights came at me. Ground fog began to drift in from the fields on either side of the highway. It began to close in over the road. I wanted to make time, and if this kept up I wasn't going to be able to make time.

Most of the gas stations I passed were dark. When I came up on a lighted one, I slowed down, tempted. I hit the gas again and went on by. It wouldn't solve anything. I could grab the attendant's car or anything he happened to be working on, but unless I buried him in his grease pit he'd pass the word on that would tie me to the new car. And even if I buried him, the presence of the Ford when I abandoned it would put the collar around my neck for anyone checking the highway from the motel on up the line.

I needed a setup that would let me run the Ford over a cliff, or the equivalent. Even more I needed to get off Highway 80. The john in a girl's dorm doesn't get any more action than that damn highway.

I went over it in my mind. Van Horn is a hundred twenty odd miles east of El Paso. A dozen miles the other side Highway 80 plows ahead due east, but Highway 90 ducks south. It looked like a better choice. I couldn't count on Jimmy's pulling the covers over his head. They could be out looking for me already.

I made it in an hour and thirty-five minutes, fog and all. I had to fight my eyes closing down all the way, and I hit the shoulder a couple of times, dozing off, but at twenty minutes to midnight I turned onto 90 and headed south. It was a narrower road, much less traveled. I began to watch for a motel. When I saw one with a car parked out close enough to the road, I'd drive a mile beyond, walk back, jump the switch on the car in the motel yard, and take off. There'd be nothing to tie the abandoned Ford to the stolen car, even if the best I could do with the Ford would be to run it off into a field.

I couldn't have been more than twenty miles in on 90 with everything around me as black as the inside of a closet when a pair of headlights came on suddenly in my rearview mirror. A red flasher started bouncing off the Ford. He must have come up behind me with his lights off, because I hadn't seen a thing. I took a quick look at the speedometer. Sixty-five. Should be no sweat there. I heard no siren, but there was no doubt he intended me to stop. He pulled out alongside, then burst ahead and cut in.

I had to jam on the brakes and cut the wheel hard to avoid scraping fenders as he herded me to the side of the road. As he went past me I could see he was in an unmarked car. I hadn't known the Rangers used unmarked cars. Live and learn.

I was ready when he walked back and leaned in the window I'd rolled down. I handed him my driver's license made out to Roy Martin. Paper-clipped to it was a twenty dollar bill. I could see a trooper hat silhouetted against the dark, but I couldn't see the face beneath it at all. I could sense rather than see him looking around the Ford's interior before he walked back to the rear and put a flash on the license.

He returned and handed it in to me. The twenty dollar bill was gone. "Drive up the highway a quarter mile," he said. His voice sounded as if he regularly had steel filings for breakfast. "Turn right the first road. A hundred fifty feet in there's a white fence. Turn left and stop. I'll be right behind you." He walked back to the cruiser. I hadn't gotten to say a word.

I could feel a slow burn coming up. If this sonofabitch thought he was going to take my twenty and then write me up anyway, he was damn well going to find out differently. When I buy someone, I expect him to stay bought.

He pulled ahead to let me out, and I eased back out on the highway. I rolled down the road slowly, watching for the first turn on the right. Even at that I almost missed it. It was hardly more than a dirt drop-off. Halfway into my turn I thought I'd made a mistake, but the headlights behind me turned in, too. I came up to the white fence, and turned left. In twenty-five yards I faced a dead-end, an impenetrable, jungle-like brush tangle dead ahead in the headlights.

I was getting hotter by the minute. I was losing time. I had missed a turn despite his directions, and wound up in this jackpot. The clearing was too small to swing around in. I started to back out. A red glow filled my rear-view mirror. I turned my head. The cruiser was backing into the clearing, sealing me in. Even as I looked he cut his lights.

All of a sudden I had a feeling.

I cut my lights and motor, fumbled a flashlight out of the glove compartment, and went out the door on the passenger's side. The unmarked car, the absence of a siren, this dead-end deserted spot he'd directed me to—

When I heard him walking I put the flash on him. He stopped dead in the beam of light. He was holding a gun, a blued-steel job. He had on a campaign hat that looked like a Ranger's hat. His clothes didn't look anything like a uniform except for the color. The bastard was no more a cop than I was.

He brought his gun up and snapped off a shot at me just as I let go at him with the Woodsman. He turned and started to run. I put one in his ankle that brought him down with a crash. He landed all sprawled out, the gun flying off in the bushes. I got over to him fast in case he had another.

When I got the flash full on him I saw it didn't make any difference. He'd been running on reflex. The hard core of the light shone down on a round, dark hole just a hair to the right of center between his eyes. The little old Woodsman might not have the stopping power of a .38, but it gets there just the same.

It was quiet in the clearing. I walked over and put the flash on the bandito's car. It was a Ford, too. It looked in better shape than mine. I got his car keys out of his pocket and got under the wheel and started it up. The engine vr-r-roomed with power. Something extra under the hood.

It looked like I had won myself an automobile.

I put on the dimmers on both cars and opened the trunks of both. I loaded his gear in mine and mine in his. I took the license plates off both cars and chopped them up with a hammer and cold chisel. With a screwdriver I worked on the red flasher on the roof until I was able to unscrew it. I knocked down the edges of the socket that held the bulb with the chisel, and slapped a square of tape over it. The black friction tape merged with the color of the car. I rummaged around through saws and climbing irons in my tool chest till I found a set of Florida plates. I put them on the new Ford.

I cleaned out my wallet and started from scratch. When I put it back on my hip again I was Chester Arnold of Hollywood, Fla. I had business cards in the wallet identifying Chet Arnold as a tree surgeon. When it pleases me I'm a tree surgeon. A good one.

When I was all set I went back for my unknown benefactor. I dragged him over and stuffed him into the trunk of the new Ford. With the tool chests already in there it was a tight squeeze, but I finally got the back deck lid closed. I took off out of there.

Out on the highway every five miles I threw a piece of chopped up license plate out the window. It helped to keep awake. Then it started to rain. It doesn't rain often in West Texas, but when it does it doesn't fool around. I hunched down over the wheel, watched the road in the streaming windshield, and pitched license fragments.

Forty miles up the highway I ran into a torn-up section under repair. In those parts they're so sure it's not going to rain they don't bother with the nicety of preserving one lane of macadam. They tear up the road from shoulder to shoulder, roll it, and drive on the dirt till they get the black-top back on. If it does rain they have a driving rodeo through four to six inches of Texas gumbo. Never let anyone tell you the Texan is not a sporting animal.

It was raining so damn hard that in less than a mile the whole graveled roadbed was solidly under water. The Ford slipped and slithered along. Even at five miles an hour a couple of times I wasn't sure I was going to make it. It was like driving across a ten mile lake. I had to watch the highway department right-of-way stakes as they glistened in the headlights alongside the road to be sure I was still in the channel.

I finally got out on hardtop again, and for the next ten miles I listened to Texas mud slurp off the undercarriage at every little jounce. From what I could see of it I could have set up a fair-sized sweepstakes selling chances of the Ford's original color. I concentrated on driving and staying awake.

When the speedometer said I was two hundred miles from El Paso, I started looking for a deep culvert. When I saw a likely looking one I pulled over on the shoulder. I got out and walked around to the back. I never saw as black a night. It was raining like someone had turned on the petcock and gone off on vacation. I was soaked in less than a minute.

I got the trunk open, and hauled out my passenger. I hoisted him over to the bank and rolled him down it. He went in with a satisfying splash. I got back in under the wheel and started slogging up the highway again. When they found him, no one would connect my benefactor to me or to much of anything else. Ditto the Ford I'd left behind in the clearing.

I'd passed Marfa and Alpine a long way back, clusters of lights in the dripping night. I was between Marathon and Haymond when I dumped the body. Twice on the long stretch between Sanderson and Del Rio I nearly went to sleep. I was driving myself as hard as I was driving the car.

Outside of Brackettville dawn was breaking in a dirty gray sky when I got a leg cramp so bad it pulled my foot clear off the accelerator. I stopped the car and got out and limped around it a couple of times, but I couldn't shake it off. I drove through town with my left foot on the gas pedal and into a motel on the outskirts. I woke up the owner, shut up his grumbling about the ungodliness of the hour, took the key he gave me and headed for the cabin he pointed out.

I figured I was about 450 miles from El Paso, and it had been a long, long day.

I shed clothes all the way from the door of the cabin to the bed, and I was asleep before I was halfway down to the pillow.

A year after I left home I was up in northern Ohio working the midnight-to-eight shift in a gas station on the edge of town. It was colder than a whore's heart up there in December, but it kept me eating. From two to seven I wouldn't average half a dozen cars. I'd sit inside with my feet cocked up on a gasoline heater, and wait for daylight.

Or listen to Olly Barnes.

He was an odd one. I couldn't figure why a good-looking

guy with a college degree should spend his time hanging around the station till all hours in the morning, talking to a kid like me. Naturally I thought he was a queer at first. Then I decided he wasn't, but I couldn't make him out. He was slender, with a pale, narrow face dominated by steel-rimmed spectacles, a high forehead, and straw-colored hair. He was about thirty. His hands were small and usually fluttered nervously while he talked. He had a beautiful speaking voice.

Two or three nights a week he'd be around the station till five in the morning. I never could see how he could keep his eyes open on his bookkeeping job. One thing I noticed about him. He talked a lot about the places he'd been and the things he'd seen, but never about the people. He talked travel, books, paintings, opera, ballet; talked with a passionate intensity. In the beginning I tried to tell him he was way over my head with most of what he had to say. When I saw it didn't matter, I shut up and listened. Olly brought me books I didn't read, and tried to hide his disappointment when I admitted it.

And then one morning the police came and took him away. It was about three thirty, and he'd been talking, as usual, when the cruiser pulled up outside. Olly's good-looking face crumpled like wet cardboard when he saw the big man in plainclothes walking toward the station door. I thought he was going to run, but if he thought of it he didn't have time.

The big man stood in the open doorway, cold air pouring in all around him. "Let's take a ride, Oliver," he said. He had a broad, flat face with high cheekbones and no more expression than an iron skillet.

"No," Olly whispered. "No!" That time it was a scream. He did start to run then, aiming at the garage area, but the man in the doorway took two steps forward and picked him off by the shirt-front like I'd scoop a fly from the wall. He half-carried, half-dragged Olly outside without saying another word. The door slammed behind them.

I went outside to the cruiser. It was none of my business, but I went out, anyhow. A uniformed man was driving. I rapped on the rolled-up front window. I could see Olly and the big man in the back seat. Olly was crying. The uniformed man lowered the window and looked out at me. "What's it all about?" I asked him.

He sat with his head cocked as if he were listening for something from the back seat. When nothing came he rolled up the window and wheeled the cruiser around the pumps and out on the highway.

I stood and watched the tail-lights diminishing up the road. It was a bitter cold night, without a star or a light of any kind, except for the lights of the station. It wasn't any of my business. And I couldn't walk off and leave the place. I went back inside, out of the cold. Olly's overcoat still lay on a chair where he'd dropped it when he came in.

Between then and seven o'clock I called the police four times. No one had ever heard of Oliver Barnes. I described the big man. They knew him, all right. His name was Lieutenant Winick. No one had seen him, either.

A little after four it started to snow. Between calls to the police I was kept busy clearing the station's driveways. By dawn there was six inches on the ground, and it was blowing hard. After seven I was too busy to call any more. When my relief came on at eight I had to stay over an hour to help with the rush of cars.

When I was able to get away there were no buses running. I put Olly's overcoat over my arm and walked the mile and a half into town. Drifts were already a couple of feet in some places, and the storm was spraying line-drive sheets of snow. Cold as it was I was sweating by the time I reached the police station. That kind of weather made heavy going.

I didn't really know what I was doing there. I guess I'd always known Olly wasn't exactly a hundred cents on the dollar. Still, a deal like that—

What if it had been me? Wouldn't I have wanted someone to at least find out the score?

I might as well have talked to a wooden Indian as the sergeant at the desk. He asked a hell of a lot more questions than he answered. Who I was. Where I lived. Where I worked. What my interest was. He finally made a pretense of checking the blotter, and said that no Oliver Barnes had been booked for anything. I knew he was lying, but for him that ended it.

I hung around. Nobody tried to run me out, but they didn't make it easy for me to stay. I tried my questions on two or three newcomers, with the same results. The heat in the waiting room kept putting me to sleep every time I sat down. At eleven o'clock I gave up. I left Olly's overcoat at the desk—in case he came in looking for it, I told the sergeant—and went home to bed.

When I woke at four it was still snowing. I dressed and walked back up to the station after getting a cup of coffee at the corner. When he saw me come in the same sergeant spoke before I could. "Lieutenant Winick wants to see you, kid," he said to me. "Inside. Second door on the left."

Winick looked up from behind his desk when I knocked and entered his office. His high-cheekboned features were just as expressionless as they'd been before. He leaned back steeply in his chair, folded his arms, and looked me over. "Stanton said you wanted to see me," he said at last. As though he'd just got the word, and I hadn't been trying since eight thirty.

"Where's Olly?" I asked him.

"In a cell. Where he belongs."

"Why? What for?"

Winick's slitted eyes were unwinking. "Your friend has a bad habit. He coaxes little girls behind buildings and takes their panties down." His harsh voice deepened as his eyes bored into mine. "*Little* girls. Seven, eight, nine. And you know what he does then?" He told me. "Like day before yesterday," he concluded. "It wasn't hard to know where to look, even without the kid's description when her mother brought her in."

The roof of my mouth felt dry. "How good—what kind of a description?"

"Oliver Barnes' description." Winick's voice blared at me suddenly. "Did you know he'd served a reformatory sentence and a prison term for the same thing?"

"No, I didn't."

"Then you know now. You're not very choosy of your company. How long've you been in town?"

"Six months. When—what time did it happen?"

The big shoulders rose and fell in an elaborate shrug. "Five, six o'clock. The kid wasn't sure."

I felt a sense of excitement. "Five or six o'clock in the evening?"

"Five or six o'clock in the evening," Winick agreed with exaggerated patience.

"Then it couldn't have been Olly," I said triumphantly.

Winick smiled. "He confessed."

"Confessed? Look, you said it happened between five and six day before yesterday?"

He was watching me narrowly. "That's what I said."

"Then it couldn't have been Olly. He brought some books over to my place at four in the afternoon day before yesterday, and he stayed talking until I went out to eat at seven. It couldn't have been Olly, you hear me?"

He stood up behind the desk. "You're mixed up on the days. It happens to you night workers. He confessed."

"The hell I'm mixed up on the days! How could he confess to something he didn't do? You—"

"Careful of the territory you're taking in, kid." Winick's voice could have cut wood. "Where do you fit in this? What kind of friend is Barnes to you?"

"Why don't you ask me what kind of friend I am to Barnes? The way I see it, I'm the one he needs. I want to talk to him."

"He's not seeing anyone. He has fits of remorse."

I could feel myself shaking. "Listen, I'll testify Olly couldn't possibly have—"

"You're going off half-cocked, kid," the hard voice cut me off again. "Did you hear me say Barnes had confessed? In detail?"

"You made him confess! He was afraid the minute he saw you. Because he did it before doesn't mean he did it this time. You must have—"

"Listen to me." Winick's voice was quiet again. "He did it. He confessed it. Can you get that through your thick skull?"

"There must be somebody else for me to talk to around here besides you," I said desperately. "You're not even listening. I tell you Olly couldn't—"

"*You're* not listening to *me*." Gimlet eyes drilled into mine. "Barnes is a menace to society. He's proved it. He should never have been out on the street. This time I'm tucking him away for a good long stretch."

"But he didn't *do* it! Not this time, anyway!"

"He did it." Winick's heavy voice was flat with authority. His eyes appeared almost closed as he looked across the desk at me. "Should I ask Barnes if you were with him?"

My hands clenched. "Is that supposed to make me run of here? By God, I know what I know. I don't care *what* he did before. This he didn't do, and I'll talk till I get someone to listen."

"You sound to me like someone fixing to get his balls caught in the machinery." Winick leaned down over the desk, resting his weight on his big-knuckled hands. "I know what Barnes is. The people in this town know what he is. When you talk to me, you're talking to all of them."

I got out of there.

I didn't believe Winick, but I found out he was right. Everyone I tried to get to listen to me gave me nothing but a blank stare. Nobody would believe it couldn't have been Olly.

And then I found out the hard way some of them weren't going to believe. The next day I lost both my job and my room. Winick had been to see my boss and my landlady. All of a sudden I was on the street with twenty-three dollars between me and the snow.

I stuck around another day, trying to get someone to listen. I was half out of my mind, crazy-mad at the town and the people in it. And at Winick. Especially at Winick. That night I slept till four A.M. in the railroad station with my head on my bag. Winick's cops found me then and threw me out. I must have ground a quarter inch off my teeth, stumbling around the slippery, frozen streets, lugging my bag. I was half frozen by the time the first one-arm coffee joint opened up.

In the cold gray light of the morning I gave up. I walked out to the edge of town and stopped a highway bus and told the driver to get me eleven dollars worth away from there. I purposely hadn't bought a ticket at the bus station because I figured if Winick wanted to keep a string on me he'd have counted on that.

I wound up across the state, a hundred eighty miles away. I got a job as stock boy in a chain grocery. Three times a week I bought a northern Ohio newspaper and read every word of it, looking for news of Olly.

It wasn't much of a surprise when I finally saw it, three months later. The black headlines said Olly had been sentenced to fifteen years.

That day I quit the human race. I never went back to my job. I've never done a legitimate day's work since. The work I've done since then has always been with an illegitimate purpose in mind. If that was the way it was, they could damn well have it that way.

I bought a gun in a hockshop. I didn't even own a car. The local paper nipped hard at police heels over the series of gas station holdups by a quick-moving pedestrian who always disappeared into the darkness.

I was surprised at how easy it was. I had only two close calls. Once I was scared off before I'd committed myself, and another time I had to stop an attendant from chasing me by shooting over his head.

The money piled up. I knew what I was going to do with it. I bought a second-hand car and learned how to drive it. About ten weeks after Olly started his sentence I drove the hundred eighty miles back across the state. Back to Winick. I rang his doorbell at ten o'clock at night. He came to the door himself. Not that it made any difference; I was all set to go right into the house after him.

I shot him in the face, four times, as he stood at the door looking out at me. He went backward in a kind of shambling trot. "That's for Olly, you bastard," I told him. I don't think he heard me. I think he was dead before his big shoulders hit the floor.

Winick was the first.

He wasn't the last.

I woke up at sundown in the Brackettville motel, humped myself across the street to a combination grocery-restaurant, and loaded up on bacon and eggs and black coffee. I re-crossed the highway and went right back into the sack. I woke up the next time at five thirty in the morning feeling better physically than I had in weeks.

I had breakfast at the same restaurant, and was ready to leave. I climbed into the new Ford, listened appreciatively to the engine sound when I started it up, and tried to back out of my parking place. The car rocked back and forth, but wouldn't budge. I sat there blank for a minute before it dawned on me what must have happened. All that Texas gumbo I'd run through—when half-dried it had frozen the brakes down tight.

Back across the road I went again. I rousted out a barefoot kid at the restaurant and brought him back with me. He crawled underneath and clawed out a couple of pecks of rich-looking mud. He had trouble freeing the emergency, but finally managed it. I tied a handkerchief on the emergency to remind myself not to use it. Those brakes wouldn't be fully dry for two or three days. I gave the kid two dollars, and he turned cartwheels all the way back to the restaurant.

It was a beautiful morning when I hit the road. After the storm everything was fresh and clear. The highway was dry and there was no traffic that early in the day. At the first straight stretch I laid down on the accelerator to see what the Ford could do. I chickened out at 105, and it felt like I had an inch left. The thing was a bomb. It held the road well, too.

I drove on through Uvalde, San Antonio, Seguin, and Luling. I had lunch in Weimar. In the afternoon I piled on through Houston, Beaumont, and Orange. I made it into Lake Charles, Louisiana, and spent the night there. The speedometer said 469 miles for the day.

I'd pushed it a little because I wanted to make Mobile the next night. In Mobile I could get guns and other things I needed from Manny Sebastian. I had to ditch the artillery I had. One gun traced back to two bank guards in Phoenix, the other to a body floating in a rain-swollen ditch. If Manny hadn't lost his contacts, I could get a Florida license and registration from him to match what I was driving.

I was out on the highway again by six thirty the next morning. Ten miles east of Lake Charles I turned north on Route 165 at a little place called Iowa. I stayed with the new route for twenty miles to Kinder, then headed east again on 190. This was the New Orleans bypass. I sailed through Eunice, Opelousas, Baton Rouge and Hammond in Louisiana, and crossed into Mississippi at Slidell. A few miles further on 190 hooked back into 90 again, and I rolled along the Old Spanish Trail through Bay St. Louis, Pass Christian, Gulfport, Biloxi, and Pascagoula. Along that sunlit stretch I was seldom out of sight of white sand and blue gulf. When I pulled into a motel in Mobile about five o'clock the speedometer said 343 miles.

I washed up, had dinner, and drove downtown to the Golden Peacock, Manny Sebastian's joint. After midnight the place really swung far out, but at this time of night it was quiet. Manny had a finger in a lot of pies. He hadn't seen me in four or five years, but he recognized me the minute I walked in. He came over and shook hands. He'd put on a lot of weight since I'd seen him last, and his jowls and extra chins transformed the face I remembered as jovially ugly into something sinister-looking.

"The back room?" he asked me with a cocked eyebrow.

I nodded. He walked over behind the bar and engaged in small-talk with two of the half dozen customers. In five minutes I saw him select a key from a huge key ring and let himself out through an unmarked door alongside one marked "Office." The unmarked door was just outside the enclosure of the bar. I gave it another couple of minutes and walked around and tapped. Manny let me in and then closed and barred the door. He had a bottle and glasses already out on the small table that was the room's only furnishing besides an old-fashioned iron safe in one corner.

"Long time, man," Manny said to me. "How's old hit-the-squirrel-in-the-eye-at-a-hundred-yards?" He walked to the table and poured and handed me a drink. "What's your problem?"

"Not the same as yours. You talk too much, Manny." I took a swallow of my drink. "How're you fixed on Florida registrations?"

He nodded. "What're you driving?"

"A Ford all over mud on your parking lot." I handed him one of my Chet Arnold cards. "Have your boy run off a license while he's at it."

Manny went to the door and unbarred it. He called someone over to whom he spoke in a low tone, and closed the door again. "Ready in an hour. Like what else?"

"Hardware. A Smith & Wesson .38 and a Colt Woodsman."

He nodded again. "I'll have to send up to the house for the Woodsman. I've got a .38 right here." He was already whirling the dial on the old safe. "I range-tested it myself. Shoots a fraction high and to the left. The Woodsman's perfect."

"You know where they came from?"

Manny looked hurt. "Right out of the factory." He produced the Smith & Wesson with a flourish, still in the original box. "Never been fired except by me, either of 'em."

"Okay, Manny. What's the damage?"

He squinted up at the ceiling. "Oh, say four hundred for the lot. Paperwork comes high these days."

I paid him. Paperwork wasn't the only thing that came high, but I had to have those guns.

"Grab a seat at the bar. On the house," Manny said, pocketing the cash. "I'll give you the office when I get your stuff together. How're things in general?" The shrewd eyes in the larded-over face studied me.

"Quiet."

He chuckled. "A hundred seventy odd thousand quiet?"

I forced my face into a smile. "I read about that. Nice touch. Sounded like Toby Coates. Or Jim Griglun."

"Toby's in Joliet," Manny said smoothly. "And Jim lost his nerve after that time in Des Moines."

"Sometimes a man gets it back."

Manny shook his head. "Not if he didn't have too much to start with." He grinned at me companionably. "Your pawprints were all over that Phoenix job. You ought to miss a shot once in a while."

Out of the mouths of fools. I made a mental note.

"Sorry to disappoint you," I said as lightly as I could manage. "I've been in hibernation." A growing feeling of irritation mounted within me. This kind of earache I couldn't use.

He seemed to sense my mood. "Who should know better?" he said, cryptically enough, and opened the door. "Order up. It's on the house, remember."

I sat at the bar and ordered a highball I didn't want. Through a window at the right I could see out on the parking lot. A slim redhead with a limp was walking around the Ford. As I watched he raised the hood, leaned in and then out, and wrote something down on a piece of paper. The engine number, I thought.

I nursed the drink for half an hour, and then ordered another. I was two-thirds of the way down to the bottom of it when Manny slid onto the next stool and laid a package down on the bar quite openly. "Eddie says that's a real fireball out on the lot," he said to me softly. "I got a wheelman would give his front teeth for it. You want to trade? I'll give you something to boot."

"Not right now, Manny. I'll keep you in mind, though." I picked up the package and went out to the car. I pulled over to a corner of the lot and unwrapped the package. I put the new license and registration in my wallet, and switched loads from the old guns to the new. I tried them for balance. They felt all right. As soon as I had a chance I'd check out the Smith & Wesson. If Manny said it was throwing a little high and to the left, it was probably more than a little.

I drove out of the lot. More from force of habit than from any real belief that someone might be following me, I doubled and twisted over a circuitous route back to the motel. The conversation with Manny bothered me. Manny was a gossip. Never to the wrong people, so far as I knew, but a gossip is a gossip. This driving around the country so soon after a job bothered me, too. Before I'd always had a nice, quiet place to hole up in between jobs. This time I wasn't calling the tune, though.

I promised myself that as soon as I got straightened out in Hudson, Florida, I'd go to earth in a hurry. Back at the motel I sacked in and slept solidly.

The next morning was the fifth day since I'd left Phoenix. I got another early start and left Highway 90 about thirty miles beyond Seminole, Florida, at Milton. On 90-A I busted along through Galliver, Crestview, DeFuniak Springs, Marianna, Chatahoochee, Tallahassee, and Monticello. I was on the homestretch now. At Capps I turned south on U.S. 19. Out in the country I picked out two swift-running rivers about fifty miles apart, and I threw the old Smith & Wesson into the first one and the old Woodsman into the second.

At four in the afternoon I saw a sign at the side of the highway: Town Limits, Hudson, Florida. I was forty or fifty miles south of Perry. I drove through the main square and found a motel on the south edge of town called the Lazy Susan. I'd covered 362 miles since morning. I registered, showered, ate at the motel, went into the lobby and worked my way through half a month-old *Time*, and went to bed early. After that stretch on the road I wanted to start out fresh in the morning.

I had breakfast in town at a place called the Log Cabin. It looked like stucco but could have been stucco over logs. It was early, but the place was busy. It looked like a factory crowd. Not much conversation, even with the good-looking young waitress who wore an engagement ring but no wedding band.

After breakfast I walked around the square. Driving through yesterday, I'd estimated the town at six or eight thousand. This morning I upped that a little. The store windows were clean, and the displayed merchandise looked fresh. There were no empty stores. The merchants must at least be making the rent money.

I walked past the still unopened bank. It was an old building, bristling in its external impression of maximum security. Like a two-dollar watch of the type that used to be called a bulldog.

I bought a local paper in the drugstore, carried it under my arm to the little park in the square, and sat down on a bench in the morning sunlight. The park faced the town hall and the post office. I looked at the post office a couple of times. To be diverted, registered mail almost had to be tampered with by post office personnel. Although of course the packaged money didn't need to have been registered yet at the time it was intercepted.

The paper turned out to be a weekly. I read every line of it, including the ads. It's a habit of mine. Tips are where you find them. I've had a subscription for years under one of my names to *Banking, the Journal of the American Banking Association*. There's a column in it called "The Country Banker," and two of the best tips I ever had came right out of that column. *Banking* used to publish pictures of newly remodeled bank interiors. Lately they've pretty much cut that out. It must have occurred to someone they were being too helpful.

In the Hudson *Chronicle* I read right down to the Help Wanted and the Positions Wanted ads. There's something to be learned about a community from each. I read all the other ads. If there was a tree surgeon in Hudson, he wasn't using the *Chronicle* to attract customers.

I folded the paper up and walked back to where I'd parked the Ford. Main Street in Hudson ran east-west from the traffic light in the square, not north-south on 19. I drove east on Main. When the stores thinned out, I slowed down. The first houses were small, with tiny yards or none at all. No work for a tree surgeon there.

A mile beyond the built-up section of town the whole area south of Main was a swamp. I remembered seeing it on a map as Thirty Mile Swamp. From what I could see of it, it was no kitchen-garden swamp, either, but a fibrous jungle of cypress and mangrove in brackish-looking water, the whole drearily festooned with Spanish moss. At the side of the road beside a shack a hand-painted sign said: AIRBOAT FOR HIRE.

I turned the Ford around and started back. Back at the edge of town again I turned north and began crisscrossing the side streets. Gradually I worked into higher ground and an improved residential area. I turned finally into a block-long street with only three houses on it. Big houses. Estates. I slowed down. This was what I needed. Property that needed to be kept up, and people with the money to pay for it. I drove around, and made notes on the edge of my newspaper.

When I'd accumulated half a dozen I headed back to the square and parked. I found a real estate office above the local five-and-dime and climbed the stairs with my paper under my arm. A young fellow hopped up from behind a desk as I entered. He had on a short-sleeved white shirt with a tie. Below the executive level in this latitude the short-sleeved white shirt is practically a uniform. Nobody wears a jacket, and after lunch the ties come off. Nobody is ever in a hurry.

"Yes, sir?" the boy said briskly. He had a nice smile. "Jed Raymond, sir. May I be of help?"

"Chet Arnold," I said, and handed him one of my business cards. "I just came in to pick your brains." I looked at my newspaper. "There's a big white Georgian house up on Sand Rock Road and Jezebel Drive." I looked at Jed Raymond. "Odd name for a street, that."

"Old Mr. Landscombe named it, Mr. Arnold. They do say he had his reasons." Jed Raymond looked up from his inspection of my card. "You want the tree work?" He shook his head doubtfully. "Mr. Landscombe died six months ago, and there's an unholy dust-up about his will. Three sets of heirs suing each other. The estate'll probably be in probate for years." The boy had a soft drawl and a mournfully humorous smile. He had a bright, heart-shaped face under a ginger-colored crewcut. Any woman over thirty would have taken him to raise and glad of the chance.

"Who's the estate administrator?" I asked him. "He shouldn't want the estate to run down."

Raymond looked impressed. "I believe it's Judge Carberry." He pronounced it "Cah'bry." "If it's not he'll know who it is. You could have somethin' there."

I wrote the name down. "How about a fieldstone rancher up on University Place and Golden Hill Lane?"

"Belongs to Mr. Craig at the bank. His daddy used to be in the lumber business. So'd Roger Craig until he had a heart attack a while back. He came into the bank then. Guess his family owned most of it, anyway."

I looked at the rest of my list and decided to skip them for the time being. A judge, and a banker. Better still, a banker who had been in the lumber business. These two looked like solid leads. If I could crack either one, I was in business in this town. "You know your real estate, son," I told Jed Raymond. "Anything in the regulations says I can't buy your lunch one of these days?"

"If I find anything I'll get it amended," he grinned. He tucked my business card into his shirt pocket. "I'll keep this, if you don't mind. I might hear of something for you."

"Fine. I'm at the Lazy Susan now. If I change, I'll let you know. You happen to have a detailed map of the area?"

He reached in a counter drawer and handed me a thickly folded-over packet. "This one's even got the projected streets in the new development east of town." He waved me off as I put my hand in my pocket. "Hope you do y'self some good locally, Mr. Arnold."

I went back down the stairs to the street. I always carry two tool kits with me, a large one to work out of and a small one for show. I walked back to the Ford and got the small one out of the trunk. I tucked two double-bitted axes into the loops on either side of the chest. When a man formerly in the lumber business saw such a kit, I shouldn't have too much trouble getting into his office.

I walked back up the street toward the bank.

I was twenty-three when I killed my second man. Funny thing: it was in Ohio, too. Massillon. Five of us had flattened the bank on the northeast corner of the main intersection, but one of the boys got trigger-happy inside. In the getaway Nig Rosen and Duke Naylor were burned down in the street before we made it to the getaway car. A mile out of town I got a deputy in a cruiser trying to cut us off. Two days later the rest of us were flushed out of a farmhouse. Clem Powers was killed. Barney Pope and I were bagged.

Barney was an old lag. He knew he'd have long white whiskers before he made it outside again, if ever. Go for yourself, kid, he said to me as we stood in the farmyard with our hands in the air. I'll back your play.

I'd left my gun inside beside Clem's body. That scored the deputy to Clem. I told the mob scene that surrounded us I was a hitchhiker who'd been sleeping in the barn when the banditos took over, and I stuck to it. True to his word, Barney backed me up. The police didn't believe it, but the jury came close. The identification putting me inside the bank was fuzzy. The guilty verdict was lukewarm.

Even the judge was leaning. I had no rap sheet. They'd checked my prints from Hell to Hoboken, and they couldn't even find a speeding charge. Two things licked me with the judge, finally. I wasn't using my family name, of course, and the probation officer couldn't get a line on me. The judge refused to believe I'd sprung full-blown from the earth age twenty-three without previous documentation of some kind. Also—and fatally—I could produce no visible means of support.

The judge cleared his throat and said three-to-five. I think he'd been considering probation. Barney Pope drew twenty-to-life. We weren't tried for the deputy. They figured they had us cold on the bank job, and on the other there was a question of jurisdiction and identification. The local D.A. didn't want to give up his own headlines by letting us go up on the other charge.

I hadn't graduated overnight to a five man bank detail. Once I'd found out which end of a gun was which, I'd come up the ladder, from filling stations to theater box offices to liquor stores—the whole bit. I worked alone until I met Nig Rosen. Nig talked me into the Massillon setup. I guess I was flattered. I was far and away the youngest of the five.

We worked four months on that job. I kept my mouth shut, and listened. Parts of it I didn't like, instinctively, it seemed. Afterward I knew I was right. Complicated action with a bunch of hot sparks was no good. Even before we were hit I'd decided that what I wanted in the future was some kind of deal I could control myself.

In the can I had plenty of time to figure how it was going to be the next time. From the middle of my second year on, Doc Essegian was my cellmate. Everyone called him The Doctor. Maybe because he was such a wise old owl. I know he was no medical doctor.

The first three months he never even said good morning to me. Then I had a little trouble with one of the screws. When I came back from solitary, Doc laughed at me. "Don't let it burn a hole in your gut, kid," he advised me. "You're even a better hater than I am, and that's saying something." After that he kind of took me over. "Life is the big machine, kid," he'd growl at me in his after-lights-out rasp. "It chews you up and it spits you out. Don't you ever forget it."

He had the most completely acid outlook on life I'd ever run across. He really knew the score. He was consumptive to his toenails, but over the years he'd given them so much trouble inside they wouldn't certify him for the prison hospital. Each day he systematically coughed up a little bit more of his lungs, and grinned and thumbed his nose. Don't bother telling me it's impossible for our prison authorities to function in any such cold-blooded manner. I was there.

If it hadn't been for Doc I'd have applied for parole when I was eligible at the end of three years. Go ahead, if you can't tough it out, he told me, but remember this: the minute you do it you're the yo-yo on the end of the string. The least little thing they don't like they twitch the line and back you come. Do the five, he urged me. Go out clean. Spit in their eye. Get a decent job, something you can't do with a parole officer checking on you every time you turn around.

You're young, Doc said to me. Develop something you can work at once in a while and show as a means of support when a prosecutor wants to put you over the jumps. Put in time on the job occasionally. Keep a name clean to work under, because when a judge hears no visible means of support, you're gone.

I'd been there already, so I knew he was right. I had an even better reason for listening to him, though. The swag from the bank job had never been recovered. I knew where it was, and Barney Pope knew where it was. Nobody else. They'd about taken that farmhouse to pieces, but they hadn't found it. At least not publicly. A man working alone could have tapped the till. That you never do know till you get back for a look.

The reason I was sure it hadn't been found officially was that every three months I had a visit from the FBI. They always came in pairs, sharp boys, smooth dressers with faces like polished steel. I used to wonder if they came in pairs to eliminate the chance of my splitting with a single man after making a deal.

Not that I ever knocked down to them. I always insisted I was an innocent hitchhiker caught up in the middle of a police-bankrobber gunfight. They knew better, but they couldn't crack me. Each time they came we'd go over the same tired old question-and-answer game about the whereabouts of the boodle. From me they got a big fat nothing.

I found out Doc was right the first time they came back after I was eligible for parole. They turned me upside down as to why I hadn't applied. I told them I liked it where I was. That was the day I moved up to the top of their list. I knew right then that as the first pigeon out of the coop I was due to get a hell of a lot of their attention the second I hit the street. When I did I wanted it to be with as few strings as possible.

I did the bit. The day I walked out of that stinking hole I didn't have to say mister to any man. And I'd made up my mind: I wasn't going back. I didn't care what it took to stay outside. I wasn't going back.

An FBI tail picked me up at the front gate. I rode with it until he got to thinking it was a breeze. The second day I triple-doored him in a hotel lobby, and lost him.

Give the devil his due. With nothing to go on but persistence, they located me at the first two jobs I found. I wasn't on parole, but I lost the jobs. They saw to that. I'll leave it to you whether they didn't want me working so I'd be driven back to the farmhouse and the swag.

I shook them for good finally by hitchhiking up into the Pacific Northwest and hooking on in a lumber camp. I never saw a town for a year and a half. The work damn near killed me at first, but I got to like it. When I came out of there I could handle a crosscut saw and a double-bitted axe with the best of them, and I could do things with a hand-gun people pay admission to see.

I drifted into tree work later on. It seemed a natural for part-time work, and for getting a close-up look at a few places I was interested in. Like banks. When I worked, I worked hard. If I couldn't promote something for myself, I had no trouble at all catching on anywhere with a crew.

It was eight years before I went back for the Massillon boodle. I didn't need the money—I'd had two good bank popovers almost back to back—but it seemed about time. The farmhouse was gone, the farm cut up into a subdivision. I had to buy a lot to do it, but I got the swag. The deed to that lot is still in a safety deposit box in the Riverman's Trust Company in Cincinnati.

In the can nights I used to read before lights-out. At first it was at Doc's insistence. Learn something, you lazy, illiterate slob, he'd say to me. He had two gods, the dictionary and the encyclopedia. I'd read aloud to him because he had incipient cataracts. He could have had them operated on, but I think he was afraid to let them work on him while he had any light left.

An encyclopedia article would start him talking. He'd been everywhere and seen everything, twice. There were no degrees from the school I attended, but I've had to be a complete jerk not to learn.

Doc had been a bank man himself. A blaster, of the old dynamite school. He had a lot of theories, but he wasn't afraid to admit the world had personally passed him by. Forget the gangs, he'd say to me. Forget the big, involved jobs that hang up on the first weak link, because there's always a weak link. Two good men is all it takes, he insisted. Smash them. Never let up on the pressure. Never take a backward step once you're committed.

I listened, and I developed some theories of my own. I worked it out down to a few decimal points while I was up in the lumber camp getting the smell of the FBI blown off me. I divorced myself for all time from the vault-blowing jobs and the armored-truck jobs and the kidnapping-the-bank-manager-and-his-wife jobs. That was the hard way. A fast, clean operation: that's what I wanted. Hit-and-run. Smash-and-grab. They'd get a look for a hundred fifty seconds, average, with the disadvantage of surprise.

When I left the west coast I drove to Atlantic City and looked up Bosco Sheerin. Bosco liked the sound of what I had to say. I was younger than he was, but I insisted on calling the play. Bosco went along with it. He was a happy-go-lucky type, anyway. We had a two year run that was peaches-and-cream. Then one night in Philadelphia the husband of the blonde Bosco had been seeing came home early. Bosco wound up on a morgue slab with foreign matter in his gizzard. I needed a new partner.

All told in eleven years I ran through four partners, but not one of them punched out on the job. They'd have been better off if I'd kept them working steadier, but how much money can you spend? I'm no big liver. I had a shack in Colorado at timberline on the road up to Pike's Peak. In June it would snow half the mornings, and in July there were still six foot drifts in the back yard. I had another place on the Connecticut River near the Vermont-

New Hampshire border. If I was there in August, I'd jump over to Saratoga and make the race meeting. I tried to spend part of every winter in New Orleans, but when the notion took me I'd settle down for a month or two almost anywhere.

When Ed Morris was killed in a drunken argument in a bucket-of-blood in Santa Fe, I went a year without turning a trick. Then one night in a tavern in Newark I met Bunny. I watched him for a month, and I liked what I saw. He could handle himself, and he had the big advantage that he could pass as a *deaf* mute. He even knew the finger-language. He'd been small-time before I picked him up, but he did as he was told. After our first job he had complete confidence in me. He was the best partner I ever had.

Bunny—

I couldn't get away from the feeling that the scorecard was going to read five dead partners in thirteen years.

I entered the latched-back doors of the Suncoast Trust Company and approached a gray-haired woman near the railing enclosing the executive desks. "I'd like to see Mr. Craig," I said to her, handing her my card. "He won't know me. If he's busy, I'll wait."

"Will you have a seat, please, Mr. Arnold?" She rose and walked to the desk of a big man in a dark suit. She placed my card in front of him and said a few words. He looked up at me just as I turned from the railing to sit down. His eyes lingered on the flash I gave him of the double-bitted axe in its straps on the side of the tool kit. I sat down to wait.

The bank exterior might have been old-fashioned, but the interior showed signs of a recent face-lifting. Indirect fluorescent lighting was bright without being harsh. The tellers' cages were behind head-high glass panels. The only bars visible were around the vault that stood in the rear with its huge door gaping open.

A safe prediction nowadays is that a bank resculpting job will result in the appearance of a lot more glass at the expense of a lot less steel. Many tellers are as approachable as librarians. They've made it a little too easy. The pendulum's got to swing the other way. These people shoving notes and paper bags through tellers' windows are beginning to get under the skin of bank personnel. To say nothing of bank architects and the bonding companies.

In the forties, knocking off a bank on a smash-and-grab was tough tissue. It will be again. It goes in cycles. Right now the thinking is positively no violence within the bank. Whatever the bank-robber wants, give it to him. Most likely it will be recovered, and if it isn't, it's insured.

Human nature being what it is, people don't always follow the script. Bank guards suddenly acquire hero complexes. So do bank customers. It's a rare banker who hasn't testified at an inquest or two concerning the last moments of just such a paths-of-glory candidate.

The only edge a pro has is in the way he plans his getaway. The amateur is more likely than not to run into the beat patrolman's arms outside the door. Once outside the load, the pro's three-in-ten chances of getting that far blossom into three-in-four of going the rest of the way.

The amounts of cash carried even by branch banks today make anything over a job or two a year an unnecessary risk. It leaves time to study an operation. Most bankers tend to become rigid in their defensive thinking. A little probing for the soft—

"Mr. Arnold?"

I looked up. The big man in the dark suit was standing at a gate in the low railing, my card in his hand. His eyes were again on the tool chest at my feet. I rose to my feet. "Yes, sir."

"I'll have to ask you to keep it brief," he said, holding the gate open. I picked up the tool chest and followed him to his desk. Up close his color was flat-white, and there were pain-lines at the corners of his mouth. He had a big lion-like head with shaggy gray hair. He was still looking at the axe, so before he could sit down I slipped it from its loops and handed it to him.

He swung it lightly in his left hand, his right unbuttoning his jacket before he remembered where he was. He rebuttoned it. "Nice balance," he said. "Feels a bit light, though."

"You're a big man, Mr. Craig."

His mouth twisted wryly. "I *was* a big man." He sat down, running a fingertip along the helve. I hadn't made any mistake in coming here; this man had seen an axe or two before. "Make your own handles?"

"Yes, sir."

"I used to, too. Except for boning and polishing them." He handed me back the axe. "What's your business with me, Mr. Arnold?"

"I'd like to clean up the trees on your place up on Golden Hill Lane, Mr. Craig. They need it."

He nodded. "References?"

"Nothing local. I've been working up around Bellingham, Washington. Ducked out ahead of the rainy season. At your convenience I'd be glad to meet you at your place and show you I know my business. You were in lumber. I couldn't kid you three minutes."

He nodded again. "Per diem or flat contract?"

"Write your own ticket, Mr. Craig. I'll do a job for you, because with your recommendation there's work in this area I should be able to get. Like the Landscombe estate."

"Be out at my place at eight in the morning," he said. He rose to his feet. "When did you get into town, Arnold?"

"Yesterday afternoon." His calling me Arnold with no Mr. in front of it was the best sign yet. I was three-quarters of the way inside the door.

"I like your style. You've rounded up your information and boarded ship here this morning before the sun's over the yardarm. We've got a breed around here doesn't move that fast. Eight o'clock," he said again.

"I'll be there, Mr. Craig. And thanks."

"Don't thank me yet." His eyes had already returned to the papers on his desk. "If you can't cut the mustard, you don't get the job. And you're right about one thing: you won't be able to fool me. See you in the morning."

"With bells on," I promised. Walking away from his desk I slipped the axe back into its straps. At the counter I caught a fat lady's eye and opened up a checking account with eighteen hundred dollars in cash.

On the way out I glanced back at Craig's desk. I felt sure he'd know about that deposit by the time I saw him in the morning. I wanted him to know. I wanted to look to him like something more than a fly-by-night county-jumper.

Around Hudson, Florida, Roger Craig's good will could be as sharp a tool as any I had in my kit.

That afternoon I called Jed Raymond's real estate office from the motel. "Chet Arnold, the tree man, Jed," I said when I had his molasses drawl on the line. "Where do you recommend I do my drinking in town?"

"There's a place north of town on 19, Mr. Arnold. Its name is the Dixie Pig, but everyone calls it Hazel's."

"The name is Chet, son. Can I get a meal there?"

"If you're not a vegetarian. Hazel's got a habit of running a side of beef between a candle and a light bulb and calling it well-done steak. You've got to watch it her steaks don't get up off the platter and bite you back."

"That's for me. See you out there?"

"Not tonight." Regret tinged his voice. "Tonight I'm doin' a little missionary work with a gal whose daddy's plannin' a development on the edge of town. Ain't it hell what a man's got to do to make a livin'? Say, how'd you make out with Roger Craig?"

"I take a test flight in the morning."

"Hurray for our side. Tell Hazel I sent you out there, Chet. Don't let her bull you around. She's a character."

"Like what kind of a character?"

He laughed. "You'll see." He laughed again, and hung up.

I took a shower, and shaved and dressed. A drink and a good steak sounded just about right. In the early twilight I drove north from the Lazy Susan. Five hundred yards beyond the business district I took my foot off the gas as a big German shepherd burst out of the underbrush and loped along the shoulder of the road in front of me. I was still trying to decide if he was going to cut across the road when a blue sedan swung around me. It must have been doing sixty-five in a thirty mile zone. The driver crossed over sharply in front of me, out on the shoulder, and hit the dog. Deliberately.

At the last second the dog either heard or sensed the car. He jumped sideways, but not far enough. Either the fender or the wheel rolled him down into the ditch. The blue sedan veered back onto the highway and roared off down the road.

I stuck my foot into the accelerator and held it there for three seconds. Then I took it off. I couldn't afford to catch that sonofabitch. If I left him lying in a ditch I could be in trouble on the project that had brought me to Hudson. I braked the Ford, went into reverse, and backed up. Maybe I could do something for the dog.

I stood on the edge of the ditch and looked down. The dog was trying to get up. He had a long scrape on his head and one leg wasn't supporting him. I reached in the car window and got my jacket off the back rest, wrapped it tightly around my left hand and forearm, and scrambled down into the ditch. The shepherd was still trying to get up. "You gonna let me help, fella?" I asked him, and held out the wrapped arm until it touched him. I had to know if he was hurting so bad he'd bite anything that came in contact with him.

He didn't bite. I moved closer, stooped down, and picked him up. He growled a little, but that's all. An animal's got to be in a real bad way to bite me. They just don't do it. He was a big dog, and it was a steep bank, but I made it up to the car and put him on the front seat. I turned around and started back to town. A guy walking on the road told me where I could find a vet.

"Shoulder sprain," the vet said when he'd gone over him on the table. "A few gashes. Nothing serious. He'll be lame for a week. Leave him with me overnight. Your dog? You ought to get tags for him."

As though on cue the shepherd reached up from the table and took my wrist in his mouth, lightly. "I'll get the tags tomorrow," I told the vet. "Give him whatever he needs."

Outside I had to stop and think where I'd been going.

I headed out north for the second time.

I had no trouble finding the Dixie Pig. It was a long, low building, encrusted with neon. No cars were parked in front although there were marked-off parking places. I followed a crushed stone driveway around to the rear and found a half-dozen cars. Evidently Hazel's customers didn't care to advertise their drinking habits to the highway.

Inside it was like a thousand others, low-ceilinged, smoke-musty, and dimly lit. The booths were empty. Six or eight customers lolled on the bar stools with their elbows on the bar. Nobody even looked around at me as I sat down.

A curtain rustled in an opening at the center back-bar, and a woman's head poked through. At the sight of a strange face she stepped in to the business side of the horseshoe-shaped bar. My first impression was that she was standing on elevated duckboards. She seemed enormous. I looked again. The back-bar flooring was on the same level as my side of the mahogany. She *was* enormous. Six feet if she was an inch, and bursting every seam of skin tight levis and a sleeveless fringed buckskin shirt that was no more than a vest. Her upper arms for size looked like John L. Sullivan's, but the skin was like a baby's. She had red hair, and a pleasantly wide mouth. She wasn't young, but she was youthful-looking.

"What'll it be, pardner?" she asked me. Her voice was a ripened contralto, deep and rich.

"You're Hazel?" She nodded. "I'm Chet Arnold. Jed Raymond sent me by. Make it bourbon and branch."

She smiled, displaying two gold teeth evenly spaced in the center of the attractive mouth. "Jed's a good kid." She turned to the bottled array behind her, and I watched the smooth ripple of muscle in her forearm as she poured my drink. I couldn't see an ounce of fat on the woman, but I'd have bet she outweighed me twenty pounds. She was the best looking big woman I'd ever seen.

She examined me frankly as she set the drink down. "Stayin' with us a while?"

"Depends," I said. "I'm prospecting. I make like Tarzan for a living, only with more equipment. I swing through the trees with an axe and a saw in my belt."

Her head was cocked to one side as she took me in feature by feature, the powerful-looking arms folded over her superb big breasts. "I'm not so damn sure you've got the face for that kind of work," she said finally. I've been in front of X-ray machines that didn't get as close to the bone as that woman's eyes.

I moved onto the offensive. "You off a ranch around Kingman, Hazel?"

The deep voice warmed. "Not bad for a guess. Nevada, not Arizona. I was raised in McGill, north of Ely. Raised? Make it roped. I get so homesick for the rimrock country sometimes I could bawl like a week-old calf."

"The planes are still flying," I suggested.

She shook her good-looking head. "I'm married to this goddam place. I just drink another fifth of my five-star shellac and forget about it. Did you want to eat?"

"Jed said you featured steak."

"Jed said right. Take your drink over to the booth there." She pointed to a corner. "I'll put the steak on the fire."

When she brought it to the booth twenty minutes later with a mound of french fries and a couple pounds of sliced tomatoes, I ate for a quarter hour without coming up for air. I mean that was a piece of meat.

I was divot-digging with a toothpick when Hazel came back to the booth. "Apple pie? Coffee?" she wanted to know.

I tested my straining belt. "Better raincheck me."

She glanced over at the bar. Everything was quiet. Standing beside me, I had my first look at her feet. She had on worked leather cowboy boots studded with silver conches. They went for one-fifty if they went for a quarter. She slid into the booth opposite me and sat down with her chin propped in her hands. Her calm inspection raked me fore and aft. "Maybe it's not the face," she decided. "Maybe it's the eyes. What do you really do for a living, Chet?"

I reached for my cigarettes, offered her one, and got two going when she accepted. "Your pa should have hairbrushed you out of asking questions like that," I told her.

"My pa never hairbrushed me out of anything I wanted to do," she answered. "Well?"

"I've been known to make a bet once in a while," I humored her.

"That's more like it," she said briskly. "A working man you're not. What's your action? Horses?"

"Horses," I agreed.

"Is that right?" She straightened up as though someone had turned on an electric current in the booth bench. "D'you remember old Northern Star? I saw him one time at Delaware Park run five an' a half furlongs in a tick less—"

So we sat and played Remember When.

It's a damn small world sometimes. Hazel's first husband had been Blueshirt Charlie Andrews, the man who bet 'em higher than a duck can fly. I'd never met him, but he'd been a pal of a friend of mine who unfortunately attracted a small piece of lead a few years back. This I did not tell Hazel.

In five minutes we found out we'd both been in Baltimore for the Pimlico Futurity in which Platter had hung it on By Jimminy, one of the last big bets the Bradley camp blew before the old gentleman checked to his last openers. We argued whether it had been '43 or '44. I held out for '44.

"I *know* it was '43," Hazel insisted. "It was my first year at the tracks. I was seventeen."

"Which makes you—"

"Never mind the arithmetic, horseman."

"—younger than I am," I finished.

Her inward look turned back down the years. "Charlie Andrews was about the ugliest man I ever knew, I guess. He stopped off for a cup of coffee in a diner in Ely where I was a waitress. He was on his way to the coast, but three weeks later he was still in the diner tryin' to talk me into sharin' it. He was about as subtle as a blowtorch, an' I was green as grass and scared to death. He'd sit across the counter from me, takin' up most of two stools—he was about five five an' weighed two-forty, an' even his ears had muscles—an' he'd say to me, 'Hazel, honey, you got a croup jus' like a thoroughbred mare. I never hope to see a bigger piece of ass.'" She shook her head reminiscently. "He married it to get it. He was a lot of all right, that Blueshirt man. Although it sure was chicken today an' feathers tomorrow livin' with him. That man would bet on anything."

Some people came in the back door, and she stood up to go back to the bar to wait on them. "Don't go away, horseman," she said over her shoulder. "I don't get a chance to talk the language much these days."

I knew what she meant. It's a special language. When Jed Raymond walked in at eleven o'clock we were still at it, re-running races of fifteen years ago. "You must have had the password, Chet," he said to me. "Our hostess doesn't usually unbend like this to the hoi-polloi."

Hazel reached up from the booth and hit him a casual backhander in the chest that nearly collapsed him. "This guy is with it, Jed," she said, leveling a thumb at me. "Where'd you find him?"

"He found me," Jed answered when he could get his breath. "Lay off that strong-arm stuff, woman, or I'll call out the militia on you." He sat down in the booth beside me. "One for the road?"

"One," I agreed. "Then I've got to get out of here. I'm making like a workingman in the morning."

Driving back to the motel twenty minutes later, Hazel's big, handsome face danced in the windshield. With her hearty laugh and golden smile she was the most woman I'd seen in a hell of a while.

For a time I'd nearly forgotten the shape of things.

It wouldn't do.

I pulled into Roger Craig's elliptical gravelled driveway at five minutes to eight. I was wearing my poor-but-honest khakis. Craig was already out in the side yard superintending a young colored boy setting up an eight-foot section of slash pine about a foot and a half in diameter. If this was the test it was going to be a joke. Slash pine is so soft I could have handled it with my teeth. Still, Craig was a native, and this was the wood he knew.

I opened the back deck of the Ford and slid out my big tool chest, and a couple of coils of rope. Craig nodded to me jovially. I could see he knew about the deposit. His manner was a lot easier. Unless I cut a leg off, I had the job. He needed the work done, and I was now a customer of the bank.

I strapped on safety belt and climbers, opened the chest and took out a pair of goggles, and unslung the lighter of the axes. "All set, Mr. Craig?"

"Whenever you're ready, Arnold."

I walked up to the pine log and tested it for balance. It

was wedged firmly. I settled myself in front of it, digging in with my heels in the soft turf. With wood like this I had no need for a long, over-the-head axe stroke. Just as well for a still stiff arm. I went at it from shoulder height, placing the cuts more with an eye to accuracy than speed. Still, a deep V narrowed rapidly as the axe rang with the mellow sound of good steel, and the fat white chunk chips flew in a solid shower. Chips were still in the air when I stepped back with the pine log in two sections. The colored boy stood off to one side with wide-rounded eyes.

"I wish I could have tried you a few years back," Craig said. There was a wistful note in his voice.

I almost made the mistake of handing him the axe. That would really have been rubbing it in on a heart attack victim. I pushed back the goggles as I caught myself just in time. "I'd have asked for a handicap," I told him. "You've got a press agent downtown. Bright young fella in the real estate office over Woolworth's. He says you could really go."

Craig smiled with pleasure. "Jed Raymond. Good boy. Knows his way around the woods, too." The smile faded. "I get damn tired of being half a man these days." He turned businesslike. "I didn't want to give you buck fever by telling you beforehand, but you were trying out for two jobs. I ran into Judge Carberry at the club last night. Drop around and see him when you finish up here." He held up a restraining hand when I would have spoken. "What do you propose to do for me?"

"I'll do it all." I waved at the driveway. "I'll shape up that low-bush Ficus and wax myrtle when I finish with the trees." I turned to the side of the house. "Just about all of it needs thinning and trimming, especially the live oaks and that shagbark hickory. See the dead limb on that sycamore? On the other side of the house you've got two bad palmettos. The one nearest the house definitely ought to come down. Maybe the other one can be saved." I ran over it in my mind. "All told, two and a half or three day's work."

He nodded. "You're the doctor." He smiled again. "Literally, by God. Jeff here will give you a hand as you go. Just waggle that axe at him when you want him to move." Jeff showed a mouthful of teeth in an expressive grin. "I'll let the Judge know he can expect to see you when you finish here."

"I appreciate it, Mr. Craig."

"Stop in and see me at the bank any time you're ready." He went into the house, and five minutes later his car eased down the opposite loop of the driveway.

I smoked my before-climbing cigarette while I walked around the yard planning the day. One of Roger Craig's forebears had had an eye for trees. There was something for everyone. In the northwest corner he had the biggest magnolia I'd ever seen. It must have gone seventy feet. He had chinquapin, sassafras, sweet gum, red birch, and mimosa. On the other side I'd seen cottonwood and aspen. He even had a chinaberry tree.

It was a bright, sunny morning, and the air felt crisp. I was established in Hudson, Florida, and my sponsorship was the best. With a start like this if I couldn't ease up on the blind side of whoever had sandbagged Bunny, then there was something the matter with me.

I climbed upstairs and went to work. Most of the morning I thinned out tops, occasionally marking a larger limb that had to go. Jeff dogged me from beneath as I moved from tree to tree, raking and burning the scut. At noon I called down to him to grab himself a sandwich. I never stop myself. In the trees food is just so much extra weight. I go right through from eight to four.

In the afternoon I tied three different weight crosscut saws to my belt, and shouldered up a coil of rope. I went to work on the larger stuff. I'd undercut it first, then rope it to the trunk and lower it carefully to Jeff standing beneath when the overcut snapped it off. I wanted no heavy drops tearing up the side of the house or scarring the lawn.

The last half hour I trimmed up stubs and daubed them with paste. I knocked it off at four sharp. I was tired, but not unpleasantly so. The arm had held up well. It was the first real day's work I'd done since I'd cased the bank in Okmulgee, Oklahoma. I'd finally decided against trying, but I'm never too much out of shape.

I packed the gear back into the Ford, told Jeff I'd see him in the morning, and headed for the Lazy Susan and a shower. In the square the traffic light caught me, and I sat there waiting for it to change so I could swing south on 19. I had to hold up for a second after it changed as a slim, redheaded man limped hurriedly across the street in front of me, against the light.

I turned the corner with a teasing tickle in the back of my mind: had I seen him before, or just someone who looked like him? When you move around the way I do, it's hard to fit faces to locations sometimes.

Then it hit me.

The last time I'd seen that limping redhead he'd been out in Manny Sebastian's parking lot in Mobile with the hood up on my car.

I turned into the first vacant parking space.

I got out of the Ford and walked back up the street.

I sat at the wobbly desk in the motel room and spread out under the light the real-estate map of the area I'd bummed from Jed Raymond. On the floor at my feet the German shepherd lay with his muzzle on his paws, his brown eyes watching me steadily. I'd stopped at the vet's and picked him up after I'd spent a fruitless thirty minutes quartering downtown Hudson in a search for the redhead I'd last seen three hundred fifty miles away. I hadn't been able to find a trace of him.

Seeing him meant the honeymoon was over for me. There was only one reason he could be in Hudson. Manny Sebastian had decided to cut himself in on the Phoenix $178,000. It wasn't very bright of Manny. I had to give it a little thought to work out just how I was going to change his mind. Because I was definitely going to change it. First, though, there was the matter of locating the stuff myself.

The shepherd's shoulder was stiff, but he could walk. The scrape on his head had been nothing serious. "How you doin', Kaiser?" I asked him. His big tail thumped the rug. His head came up, and his new tags glistened on his new spiked collar. A twenty dollar bill had straightened me out with the motel proprietor over the added starter in the unit. It wasn't his busy season, so he could afford not to give me an argument.

I turned to the map. Finding the sack with the money in it had suddenly taken on a priority. Since seeing the redhead, I couldn't take this thing in second gear. Slow and easy was out. I had to get moving. I knew Bunny wouldn't have dug himself in too far out of town, but he wouldn't have set up a tent in front of the city hall, either. He liked to batch it alone where he wouldn't attract attention. It was one of the things I'd liked about him.

Looking at the map, I tentatively ruled out the north-south stretch of U.S. 19 above and below the square as the least likely section for Bunny to hole up in. Too much traffic. Too many people. That left Main Street east from the traffic light. And because of Thirty Mile Swamp to the south, it left Main Street to the north. I took a pencil and marked lightly—beginning at the edge of town—two points five miles apart, as close as I could figure it by the map scale. If I drove up every road leading north off Main in that stretch, I might not find Bunny but I might find a blue Dodge sedan with Arizona plates. An automobile is harder to dismaterialize than you'd think. Even the burned-out skeleton of a car would be a starting place.

I looked at my watch. I still had an hour of daylight. "Come on, boy," I said to the shepherd. He was up at once, hobbling but expectant. Out in the yard he was ready to jump up into the front seat when I opened the car door. I picked him up and put him in. "We'll pamper you for a day or two," I told him. He nuzzled my arm and sat down, dignified as a college president.

I went around to the trunk and hauled out knee-high boots, a machete for underbrush, and a steel-shafted number 3 iron for snakes. I'd seen enough of the side roads around Hudson to know I'd be doing as much walking as riding. I'd cover every cowpath a car or a man could get over in that five-mile stretch, and if that didn't turn up anything, I'd mark off another five-mile stretch and do it again. I'd cover it a yard at a time, if I had to. Whatever it took to do it, I was going to find Bunny.

We drove out Main, out of town, Kaiser sitting up to the window as steady as a sergeant-major on dress parade. He had a big head and a wicked-looking mouthful of teeth. His coat was mostly gray, flecked with brown in front. He looked all business, sitting up there.

The first two roads I turned up weren't bad. The third one I took one look, pulled the Ford in off the road, and changed to the boots. I didn't have enough daylight left to do much that night, but I wanted to get the feel of it. In the first hundred yards I found out I had a bull by the nose. Clouds of gnats and mosquitoes dive-bombed me. I lunged through knee-deep brush, chopping steadily, perspiration streaming, only the signs of recent car passage luring me on to end-of-track. When the ruts petered out by an abandoned tarpaper shack I turned around and slogged my way back.

I came out on the road again to find a two-tone county cruiser pulled in behind the Ford, and Kaiser showing a handsome set of fangs to a uniformed man trying to look into the front seat. My brush-crackling progress announced me, and the man turned to look me up and down.

"Deputy Sheriff Franklin," he said curtly. "You'd better keep that damn wolf on a leash." I said nothing. Franklin was a stocky man with a red face of the type much exposed to weather. His gray uniform trousers had red piping on the sides, and his khaki shirt was open at the throat. "What's your business out here?" he asked me.

"I'm a timber cruiser," I said.

"You're a what?"

"I'm scouting the area looking for a stand of second-growth black maple I hear is in here."

He scowled. "We're two hundred miles too far south for black maple. If you know your business, you know that." He glanced in at the weedy-looking trees shooting up in an area that had been viciously slash-cut years before.

I shook my head firmly. "I had a drink the other night with an old-timer who told me they took a million feet of black maple out of here fifty years ago. Should be a buck in it today for the guy that finds the right spot, if the slash hasn't been burned over." Franklin was studying me. "I'm doing a job of work for Mr. Craig and Judge Carberry back in town," I added.

Whatever he'd been going to say, the names stopped him. He wasn't the type to bow out gracefully, though. He swaggered around to the rear of the Ford and made a production of taking down the license plate number. "We keep an eye on these badlands," he said gruffly, and stalked back to the cruiser. He backed out on the road at fifty miles an hour, punched the shift panel on the dash, and roared down the road, wide open.

I changed back to my cordovans, put boots, machete, and golf club back in the trunk, and patted Kaiser's big head as I got back into the Ford. "Good dog," I told him. He rrrrrr'd deep in his throat, and nipped at my arm. I had a feeling Kaiser and I understood one another about uniforms.

It was full twilight when I got back to the motel.

I began to make it a habit to eat my evening meal at Hazel's. Jed frequently joined me, and we'd sit over a drink and talk, and when the bar wasn't busy Hazel would join us.

Like a lot of salesmen I've known, Jed was a complete extrovert. In a roomful of people he'd crawl onto Hazel's lap and talk baby-talk to her. He had a high-pitched, infectious laugh that turned every head in a room. With all that he was a sharp-witted kid who looked in both directions before crossing the street.

Between them Jed and Hazel knew every living soul for fifty miles. I sat and listened while they rattled family skeletons past and present twenty to the dozen. Early in the game I introduced the subject of the post office. They shook a few feathers loose from that bird, but I couldn't see anything meant for me.

Lucille Grimes was the postmistress, widow of a former postmaster deceased five years. Jed said the town couldn't understand why she didn't remarry, since she had suitors and to spare. He also said zestfully that she was a tall, leggy, cool-looking blonde.

Hazel had her own ideas as to why the beauteous Lucille hadn't remarried. She hinted darkly that the favored suitor already had a wife. Since Hazel, minus her usual spade-is-a-shovel outspokenness, failed to name him, I deduced that he was a Dixie Pig customer. From Hazel's attitude, Lucille Grimes was not one of her favorite people. Jed kidded her about it.

In all of it there was nothing for me that I could see, but that post office bothered me.

It took me eight working days to clean up the Craig and Landscombe properties. Evenings I got out and plowed up the side roads on the north side of Main, and discovered nothing. When I finished with the Craig and Landscombe places, nobody remarked on the fact that I didn't seem to be knocking down any stone walls looking for more work. The sun coast of Florida is an easygoing neighborhood.

Jed led an active social life, even for a young fellow his age. The nights he didn't show up for dinner, after a couple or three times of my eating alone, it came to be understood that if I'd postpone my own meal to seven thirty, Hazel would serve us both in the corner booth. Over coffee and cigarettes we'd sit and swap lies about horses and horse-players we'd known.

The big girl was comfortable to be around. Once in a while she'd have to get up and tend bar, but not too often. She did her real business from nine thirty to midnight. At the tracks she'd seen them all from Ak-Sar-Ben to Wood-bine. She didn't go back as far as I did by a dozen years, but as the evenings passed it was odd to see how many times we'd been in the same town at the same time. She'd seen Papa Redbird win the Arlington Classic in '48, and Rough'n Tumble the Santa Anita Derby in '51. So had I. She'd seen Turn-To win the first Garden State, and she'd been in New Orleans the winter old Tenacious first took charge. So had I. It wasn't the biggest club in the world.

Jed warned me Hazel could be moody, and her drinking a problem. I saw no sign of either. With me I think she had a chance to let off steam that had been a long time bottled up. Blueshirt Charlie Andrews had died five years before of a heart attack. Hazel had rushed into and out of a no-good second marriage, the only legacy of which was the Dixie Pig.

I liked her. I could tell she had guts. I knew she'd spit in the eye of the devil himself.

I enjoyed it, sitting around batting the breeze about the old days, but way down deep inside I was getting restless.

It wasn't what I had come for.

We were sitting in the corner booth one night, waiting for Jed. Hazel, as usual, was talking horses. Like all horseplay-ers, she had strong opinions. Arguing, she'd get excited; her eyes would flash, and she'd pound the table.

She held out for Citation as the best she'd ever seen. I was on the coast the summer Citation couldn't get past Noor in the stretch four straight races. I know he'd been away a year, and I know he wasn't what he had been. Re-gardless, I've never since been able to make him the best.

I go with Count Fleet. He didn't beat horses, he murdered them. I saw him win the Walden at Pimlico by thirty lengths. Look it up. Thirty lengths. And don't ask me who he beat. He beat the best there was around. No horse can do any more. When he came out of the far turn with his mane and tail streaming and the rest of them nowhere, it was enough to stop your heart.

It's been one of my secret sorrows that he never bred anything approximating himself as a runner. Stake winners, yes, but no Count Fleets. I think now the big horse will come from one of his fillies. If I owned a Count Fleet filly, all the gold in Fort Knox couldn't buy her. Some one of these days a broodmare by him is going to throw a jimdandy.

The forum broke up when Jed came in. He sat down, and Hazel went out back to start the steaks. The bar became busy with before-dinner thirst quenchers and she didn't come back. Everyone came in the back door. As far as I could see Hazel could have nailed up the front door and never lost a nickel's worth of business.

Jed was in high good humor. "Made a sale today," he informed me. "Drink up, drink up. I'll buy you one. Got to keep the money of the country circulatin'."

"You can buy me a brandy after dinner," I told him. I could see I'd lost his attention. From his side of the booth he could look out over the back parking lot, and he was leaning forward to look more closely.

"Well, well, well," he said softly. "Here's company for us." He stood up, a bright, artificial smile pasted on his face as a tall blonde walked in the back door. "Here's Miss Lucille now," he said loudly enough to be heard by her. "Maybe she'll have a drink with us." He moved out of the booth.

I could hear his laughing cajolery as he intercepted her in the middle of the floor. In seconds he was leading her to our booth. "—Ol' Chet's been admirin' your post office, especially the fixtures that aren't government issue," he was saying. He winked at me as I rose. "Lucille Grimes, Chet Arnold. Chet's a tree surgeon, Lucille." He grinned at her. "I don't need to introduce you in your official capacity. Chet knew who our beautiful postmistress was fifteen minutes after he'd hit town."

"Won't you sit down, Miss Grimes?" I offered, to cut off the flow of words. She murmured something and slid into the booth opposite me. Her face was cool-looking and composed under the blonde hair. Her face was a bit too long and pointed from brow to chin, but with good features. Her skin was pale, and her eyes surprisingly dark for her low-keyed complexion. Despite the lack of high points, there was nothing washed-out in her appearance.

Jed pushed in beside her and called for drinks. Lucille Grimes folded slim, capable-looking hands on the booth table and looked at me directly. "I hear you're a very capable workman, Mr. Arnold," she said. Her voice was low-keyed, too. No stress or strain.

"Thank you, Miss Gr—"

"Hear, hear," Jed interrupted. "Lucille, meet Chet. Chet, meet Lucille. What's all this Mr. an' Miss business?" He stood up and advanced on the jukebox in the corner. He fed it coins and punched buttons indiscriminately. "Dance?" he offered Lucille, returning to the booth. "Illegal, but the custom of the country," he grinned down at me. He returned his attention to her. "Join us for dinner? Private little celebration of mine."

"Another time, thanks." She sounded genuinely regretful. She danced with Jed. She danced with me. I'm not much of a dancer, but she followed me easily. She wasn't nearly as willowy as I'd thought seeing her come in the back door. She filled a man's arms. I tried to guess her age. Thirty, maybe.

I was on the floor with her when the back door opened again to admit a stocky man in gray uniform trousers with red piping on the side and a khaki shirt open at the throat. My friend from the road the other day, I thought, recognizing the blunt red face. He sat down at the bar and ordered a beer.

After another dance with Jed, Lucille excused herself. "It's been very pleasant," she said to both of us. She smiled at us impartially, gathered up gloves and bag, and exited through the rear door. Three minutes later the stocky man left his half-finished beer and followed.

Jed watched me take this in. "They're not usually that obvious, Chet. That's Bart Franklin, one of our risin' young deputies. Known as Blaze, due to a well-advertised short temper. I'm a jack-leg deputy around here myself in emergencies. Blaze isn't one of our better-loved members. He's gone for the blonde widow."

"Thanks, son. It always helps to know if another dog's after the same bone."

"You go for her?" he asked in a half-protesting tone. "I brought her over because I remembered you asked about her the other night, but—" He shook his head. "It's all yours, man. Yours and Blaze's. I tell you that gal spooks me. Somethin' about her just—"

"Nothing another ten years wouldn't help you to handle," I told him as he sat there wagging his head. The conversation died as Hazel brought the meal. Jed left at eight thirty to keep a date, and I said so long to Hazel shortly afterward.

I drove back to town, parked in the square, and went in to my act. A week ago I'd marked off four taverns as the type most likely to have attracted Bunny's trade. Every night I stopped off in two of them for a glass of beer. I'd sit in each for half an hour, exchanging an occasional word with the bartender. They all knew me now when I came in, and had my beer drawn before I said a word.

Starting with the friendliest, in another few days I'd throw each of them the same bait. "What's become of that big, dark, quiet fella used to be in here around this time of night?" I'd ask them. "Haven't seen him lately."

They'd try to remember. A bartender's customers come and go. "Oh, yeah, the big guy," I hoped one or more of them would say, "That's right, he hasn't been around, has he?"

If they remembered him, I might get a lead. I needed a lead, badly. I was on my second five-mile stretch of side roads, and I'd found nothing. If a bartender even remembered the direction Bunny drove off whenever he left the tavern, it would be more than I had now.

I couldn't racket around this town asking for Dick Pierce. A small town is wired together so tight it would be sure to get back to the interested party. Of course if I crapped out all around the green-covered table trying to find Bunny, a direct inquiry was my ace in the hole.

The day I asked, though, I had to be ready for anything.
I wasn't planning on it.
Not yet.

The next night I was making the second of my tavern
stops when the limping redhead made a mistake. He
didn't know it was a mistake, because he didn't know I'd
seen him in Mobile. I'd just climbed out of the Ford, ready
to go inside for a beer I didn't want, when he cruised by in
a black sedan at about eight miles an hour. I got a good look
at him. He didn't turn his head to look at me. He just went
on by. The sedan turned the corner above the tavern, and
pulled into the curb and stopped. I could tell by the reflec-
tion from the headlights. I knew the redhead was tailing me
as plainly as if he'd written me a letter.

I went on inside and had the beer, talked a little baseball
to the bartender, Bobby Herman, and gave some thought to
the redhead. The minute I'd seen him on the street the day
before I'd decided he was a luxury I couldn't afford. That
left two things to be settled: finding out if he'd already reported back to Manny Sebastian where he'd followed me
to, and how I was going to get rid of him.

I said goodnight to Bobby Herman and went back outside
to the Ford. I pulled ahead and turned the same corner the
black sedan had turned. There wasn't a car in sight, parked
or moving. I circled the block twice without seeing a thing. I
was just beginning to get a good mad on at myself for having
lost him again when car headlights picked me up from about
thirty yards behind me. I don't know where he came from.
The sonofabitch was good. Tailing a man in a car without
calling attention to yourself takes ingenuity. This boy had it.

I took him back uptown and east on Main from the traffic
light. Out on the edge of town I settled down to a steady
fifty miles an hour. I was in no hurry. Somewhere out in the
boondocks I'd find a place to leave him, permanently.

In the first five miles I found out how he'd been able to
follow me all the way down from Mobile without my get-

ting wise. He was an artist with an automobile. When he had room to maneuver he didn't just lock himself onto my taillight and leave me to wonder eventually about the lights in the rear-view mirror that remained the same distance behind. There was only a sliver of moon, but he rode some straight stretches with his lights out. For short distances he'd be bumper-to-bumper with me, and then I wouldn't see him at all for miles. Twice he passed me, once doing about eighty, only to pick me up again from behind. The first time he went by I wasted a look at his license plate. It was carefully, unreadably mud-spattered.

Twenty five miles up the line I came out of the woodsy darkness enveloping the road into a sleepy-looking, wide-place-in-the-highway town with a blinking yellow light at an intersection surrounded by darkened storefronts. The only other illumination was a lighted telephone booth on the main street, just before the blinker. I turned right at the intersection, right again at the next corner, and right again at the next. I was out of the car and sprinting down an alley between two stores before the redhead's headlights turned the last corner and cruised down past the Ford.

The last time I'd parked he'd turned the next corner and pulled in. I was gambling he'd follow a pattern. If he did, I had him in my pocket. I cut left through a bisecting alley, running for the main street.

I was in time to see his headlights arc around as he swung the corner. Sure enough, his car went past me and stopped not fifteen feet from the phone booth. He'd cut his lights before he even stopped rolling. He'd seen I wasn't in the Ford when he went by. In his own mind he could be getting close to the payoff. He was, but not the kind he expected. He climbed out in a rush, took a quick look around the silent town, and started to head back up the street to the corner he'd just turned. He didn't want to lose me.

He didn't.

I stepped out of the alleyway and intercepted him, the Smith & Wesson in my hand. "Hi, Red," I said to him. "How're things in Mobile?"

It would have stopped the average man's heartbeat. This was a different breed of rooster. Even in the poor light I could see him straightening his face out as he went in to a deadpan look. "You got me wrong, Jack," he protested.

"Walk up to the phone booth," I told him. I wanted to see his face in the light when I asked him the question that was bothering me. I followed right behind him, shoving the gun under my armpit. "Get inside it," I said when he reached the booth. "Make out you're dialing." He took down the receiver before he turned to look out at me. "Don't make the mistake of putting your hand in your pocket for change."

"You're makin' a big—"

"You must be the wheelman who wanted the Ford," I cut him off. "Manny tell you you could have it if you kept tabs on me for him?"

It must have rocked him, but he didn't lose his nerve. "I don't know any Manny," he said sullenly. "You off your rocker?" He was eyeing me, wondering where the gun had gone. He had a thin, pale face with a scattering of freckles.

"Have you called Manny since you followed me into Hudson, Red?"

He dropped all pretense. "Manny says you're a tough boy," he sneered. "You don't look so tough to me."

"One more time, Red," I told him softly. "Have you called Manny since—"

"Up, with a meathook, buster!" Red snatched the booth door closed with his left hand while he went for the gun in his shoulder holster with his right. His hand was still on its way under his lapel when I put one in his chest and one in his ear. Both of them took chunks of booth glass before they took chunks of Red. He did a slow corkscrew to the booth floor, the freckles stark in his white face. I emptied the Smith & Wesson into the booth, spraying it from top to bottom. I put the last one into the light. Nobody was going to call this one a sharpshooting job.

I went up the alley at a good clip and right-angled back to the Ford. I reversed it up to the next corner without putting my lights on, then retraced the way I'd driven in there. I put my lights on just before I hit the blinker. Lights were popping on in houses here and there as I swung left and headed for the Lazy Susan.

With the booth light out they'd be a while finding Red. When they did, they'd be another while trying to unscramble the jigsaw. I put the Smith & Wesson on the seat beside me in case I had to pitch it if anything came up behind me. I held it down to fifty all the way back. I only passed three cars on the way, and nothing passed me. Kaiser greeted me at the motel-room door. He stretched out at my feet and watched for twenty minutes with only an occasional blink as I cleaned, oiled, and reloaded the Smith & Wesson.

I didn't know whether Manny knew where to find me or not. I knew that if he didn't, he wasn't going to.

I went to bed.

On my next trip out to the Dixie Pig I took Kaiser along with me. There was the usual sprinkling of a dozen cars parked out in back, including Jed Raymond's sports car. I went in with Kaiser padding sedately along beside me, and Jed waved from a booth. I was two-thirds of the way across the floor before I saw Lucille Grimes with her back to me in the booth opposite him.

Jed, with his fey grin, tried to maneuver me into sitting beside Lucille. I pushed him over and sat down beside him. "Good evening, all," I greeted them.

Lucille smiled but didn't speak. Jed reached under the table to pat Kaiser who sat down beside me. I watched closely but Kaiser didn't take any offense. "Hi, there, big boy," Jed said to him. "Who's your gentleman friend, Chet?"

"Kaiser, meet Jed," I introduced them. I noticed that the blonde's long legs were as far withdrawn beneath the booth as she could manage. Evidently Lucille wasn't an animal lover. "Well, folks, what's the chief topic of conversation?" I inquired.

"The star-spangled, unmitigated dullness of life in a small town," Jed answered promptly. "Right, Lucille?"

Her thin smile was noncommittal. "I don't believe I have too many complaints," she said. "And perhaps Chet hasn't always lived in a small town."

Jed got me off that hook. "They're all small," he asserted. "The biggest of them are small, even New York City. How much town can you live in? Outside of a couple of blocks near where you work and a couple of blocks near where you sleep, the rest is as strange as to a visitor from Beluchistan. I'll take little old Hudson."

"Which side of the argument are you on, anyway?" Lucille wanted to know. "You're complaining about dullness, but you'll take little old Hudson. Page the Chamber of Commerce." I thought she looked tired. There were dark circles under her eyes. She kept watching the parking lot through the booth window. So did I, but not as obviously. We hadn't long to wait. A two-tone county sheriff's department cruiser swung slowly through the lot and down the driveway on the other side. The blonde gathered up her gloves and bag. "You'll have to excuse me, gentlemen," she said, rising. "Good night."

"For a guy slaverin' for blonde meat you don't move very fast," Jed accused me when she'd gone.

"You young sprouts just don't understand the logistics of my generation," I told him. "Our theme song is 'But They Get There Just The Same.' Pay attention; you could learn something. Your technique is all wrong."

"Not since I got out of high school it hasn't been," Jed asserted cheerfully. He turned serious. "Listen, don't let me needle you about the widow. She's—well, there's better fish in the creek. Whyn't you let me slip you a number or two from my little black book?"

"Just because a county cruiser circles the parking lot?" I asked him.

He nodded. "So you saw it, too. Blaze Franklin—" Jed hesitated. "Blaze is a little bit primitive. You know? Rednecked all the time. Who needs it to get involved with a thick turd like that?"

"So he's the jealous type."

"In spades, he's the jealous type." Jed pushed his glass around in the wet circles on the table top without looking at me. "I've heard some stories about Blaze." He turned to grin at me. "Some of them might even be true. Hey, Hazel!" he hollered over to the bar in a quick change of subject. "Bring on the fatted calf!"

We ate diligently, with Jed feeding small cuts of his steak to Kaiser, who accepted them with dignity. "You'll spoil him," I told Jed.

"He can stand spoiling. That's a lot of dog. I like his looks." He glanced at his watch. "Say, I got to get going."

When he left I sat around waiting to see if Hazel was go-

ing to be able to get away from the bar long enough to sit
down. I got a surprise when she did. The first thing I noticed was that she was wearing a dress. She must have
changed since she'd served us. It was the first time I'd seen
her in anything but the skin-tight levis. Her hair looked different, too. She'd done something to it.

"What's the occasion?" I asked her as she unloaded the
tray she'd brought over. I took another look when she set a
drink down on her side of the booth table, too. I'd never
seen her take a drink before.

"No occasion." Her voice sounded husky. "Every once in
a while I take a notion to give the animals something to
think about besides my ass." She plunked herself down
across from me.

Now that I was looking at her, her eyes indicated that the
drink in front of her wouldn't be her first for the day. I remembered Jed's warnings about her drinking. I wondered
if the storm signals were up.

She wouldn't have appreciated it, probably, but I decided I
liked her better in the levis. They suited her, somehow. In
the western ensemble she was the most female-looking
mammal I'd seen in a long time. I wasn't the only one to notice it. Every once in a while a half-splashed customer would
get carried away by the levis and acquire a sudden biological
urge. Hazel fractured the house every time with her rebuttal.
"What's with you, fella?" she'd pounce on him in that deep
voice, half purr, half growl. "Your insurance paid up? Nobody told you I got my own cemetery out in back for wise
guys snatchin' a feel?" Hazel was no shrinking violet. It took
a hardy ego to survive that little speech with the speaker
looking down on the red-faced snatcher from an average two
to four inches superior height.

Hazel tossed off her drink in a swallow and accepted my
light for her cigarette. She still had on her cowboy boots,
and the heel of one tapped steadily. Kaiser's ears pricked
forward as he lay on the floor beside me.

"I need another drink," Hazel announced. She continued
right on without waiting for me to reply, if I'd been going
to. "I'm not a blonde, but whatever she's got I'll double
and throw away the change. I'll be closing up at twelve fifteen tonight. Come back and pick me up."

I opened my mouth, and closed it again. "Twelve fifteen," I said finally.

She nodded, ground out her cigarette in the ashtray, and got up and went back to the bar. She didn't come back.

I had time to kill. On the way into town I thought about Hazel. I liked her. She was easy to talk to. She had a caustic good humor. Despite the gold teeth, when she took the trouble to fix herself up she was a damn handsome woman.

But—

Ahhh, what the hell, I told myself. Play the hand the way the cards are dealt. What did I have to lose?

I backed off in a hurry from that bit of bravado. I knew what I had to lose.

I stopped in at Bobby Herman's tavern. He was the friendliest of the bartenders on my night beat, and I was just about ready to pull the trigger on a few questions to him. As soon as I walked inside I knew it wasn't going to be tonight, though. Blaze Franklin was sitting up at the bar. Must have been a short date. So much for dark circles under the eyes.

He saw me come in, but it took him five minutes to make up his mind to do anything about it. He got up from his stool finally, two-thirds of the way up the bar from mine, swaggered past the half dozen other customers in the place, and pushed himself in on the stool beside me, his elbows out wider than they needed to be. "Don't b'lieve I've heard your name," he said in a loud voice.

"Arnold," I said. That's all I said.

"Understand you're quite a dancer," he informed me after waiting to see if I was going to continue. I wondered how much of his tomato face was due to weather and how much to alcohol. Around us the little bar-room conversations had died out. He wasn't satisfied to accept my silence. "I see you peart near ev'y day out thumpin' around that bresh out yonder," he said to me. "You keep it up you're gonna put your number 12 down on a still some day an' git your head blowed off."

"I carry a spare."

He didn't get it for a minute. When he did, he clouded over. "You in town for long, Arnold?"

"Depends," I said.

He took a long breath as though holding himself down. "Depends on what?"

I turned around on my stool until I was facing him. "Depends on me," I told him. I looked him up and down for five seconds, and returned to my beer. He put his hand on my arm. I looked down at the hand, and then at him. He removed the hand, his face flushing darkly. I knew the type. He wanted to lean on me just to show he could. I could feel the short hairs stiffening on the back of my neck. It was crazy. This bastard rubbed me completely the wrong way.

Whatever he'd been thinking of doing, he changed his mind. He got up and stalked out the door. Around me the conversation was not immediately renewed. Bobby Herman came sliding down the bar, his long arm going in concentric circles with a dirty bar rag. He was a thin-faced, pimply specimen with lank hair. "That's Blaze Franklin," he said almost apologetically. "He's a little—quick. What was that about dancin'?"

"Haven't the faintest notion," I said. I wasn't supposed to know the blonde was his playmate. Outside we could hear the roar of the cruiser as Franklin petulantly gunned it away. "Quick, huh? Who's he buried?" And as the words hung in the air, I told myself to cut it out. Trouble you can't use. Where are your brains, man?

Herman's laugh was a cackle. "That's a good one. Who's he buried?" He looked up and down the bar to assure himself of a maximum audience. "Well, no one he's stood trial for," he grinned. It was his turn to listen to the sound of his own words in the musty room. His grin faded. "I mean an escaped convict or two—things like that," he amended it hastily. He sloshed the bar rag about with renewed vigor. "Blaze's one of our best young deppities." Having—as he felt—retrieved the situation, he favored me with another smile.

I finished my beer and got out of there. I killed a couple of hours reading at the Lazy Susan, and left Kaiser in the room when I went out again. When I turned into the driveway of the Dixie Pig the lights were out in front except for the night-light. Around in back there was only one car. Hazel's car. She must have been standing just inside the back door waiting for me, because she came out and turned the key in the lock just as I pulled in.

"Let's use my car," she said. She went directly to it and got in on the driver's side. I climbed out of the Ford and walked over and got in beside her. She spun the wheels in the crushed stone backing up.

On the highway she turned south. Past the traffic light in town she leaned on it. She had a heavy foot, but she was a good driver. I watched alternately a full moon off over the gulf and the road unwinding in the headlights. There was no conversation. Sometimes I know ahead of time, but tonight wasn't one of those times.

Fifteen miles down the road she turned left on a dirt road she had to know was there or she couldn't have seen it. About a mile in on it she turned left again, and we bumped along over deep ruts for three hundred yards until a log cabin showed up in the headlights. Hazel switched off the car lights and we sat there and looked at the cabin in the moonlight. "I built most of it myself," she said. "And I mean I drove the nails. Come on."

She was out of the car and up on the little porch and had the door unlocked and open before I had the car door closed on my side. "Well?" she challenged me softly when I came up beside her. "It's a goddam good thing I'm shameless enough for both of us. You weren't going to ask me out. Why?"

"When I think of a good answer, I'll let you know," I told her. She led the way inside and closed the door behind me. I heard the snick of a bolt. In the moonlight that was the room's only light I couldn't make out many details except that the place was furnished.

Hazel came up behind me and dropped her hands down on my shoulders. "Get into something cooler, horseman," she said. She walked into the next room.

I undressed slowly. When I padded in barefoot she was buck naked on the full-sized bed. She could have been the model for all women for all time. Her eyes were closed.

I knelt on the edge of the bed. "Hazel—" I began.

She opened her eyes. Even in the semi-darkened room I could see the golden smile. "Don't you try to tell me I've gone and emasculated you," she said softly. "Come on here to me. You're a man. You'll do all right."

When it became apparent even to her some time later that

I wasn't going to do all right, she sat up on the bed. "Get me a cigarette, Chet, will you?" she asked me. She sounded tired. I went back out to my clothes and found my cigarettes. In the glow of the lighter she studied my face. "Is it me, Chet?"

"It's not you."

"You're not a queer." She said it as a statement but with an implied question.

"I don't think I'm a queer," I said.

"But this happens? Often?"

"About half the time."

She blew out a convulsive lungful of smoke. "You shouldn't have done it to me, Chet." Impulsively her big hand closed on mine. "I'm sorry. It was me who did it to you, wasn't it?" The bed creaked under her weight as she changed position. "What do you think it is?"

"Everybody's got his own opium for that sort of thing, I guess." I stubbed out my own cigarette. "Years ago I saw a cartoon in a magazine. A slick-looking battalion is marching along in perfect cadence except for one raggedy-assed, stumble-footed guy out of step with a rock-faced sergeant alongside him giving him hell. The tag line underneath has the out-of-step character telling the sergeant he hears a different drum. The inference being that he can't help it if the rest of them are out of step. That's me. I march to a different band."

"What's the music?" she asked me directly.

"Excitement," I said after I caught myself. I'd nearly blurted out the truth. I'd nearly said "guns." With the air crackling with tension and a gun in my hand I'm nine feet tall and the best damn man you ever saw, right afterward. There's another time, too, but I'm not so proud of that.

"Well, I've read about bullfighters," Hazel said philosophically. "And I've seen gamblers who were on-again off-again with women, particularly when they were losing." She stood up from the bed and walked to the chair where she'd left her clothes. Her superb big body glistened in the moonlight that filtered into the bedroom. She thought of something else and walked over to me and tapped me on the chest with a solid finger. "Forget it, man. Before we take that fence again I'll have my jukebox man wire you up with

'Yes' and 'No' buttons." The attempt at lightness hung in the air between us. Hazel punched me in the ribs. "Let's just scratch tonight from the results, horseman."

But it was a quiet ride back to pick up my car.

In my time I've had a lot of quiet rides.

At the Dixie Pig the next night I couldn't see any change in Hazel's attitude. There was no reference to the previous evening. I hadn't gone there expecting to find the details of the disaster soaped in on the back bar mirror, but I'm old enough to know it makes a difference and that the difference usually shows. I couldn't see any change in her at all. Hazel wasn't big only in her physical dimensions.

"I hear you're picking on our poor little deputy sheriffs now," she said to me, sitting down in the booth.

"Your hearing's pretty damn good, except that you've got the story all wrong," I told her.

"Not many secrets in this town," she assured me. "Especially not many that take place in taverns." She studied me as I sat there. "You could be underestimating Blaze Franklin, Chet."

It irritated me. "I'm not over or underestimating him. I don't give a damn about him."

"Don't get narky. I'm telling you for your own good. He's dangerous."

"So how come a dangerous man is a deputy sheriff?"

"I don't think anyone around here had the whole picture on Blaze until he had the uniform. It's the badge that makes him dangerous, the leeway it gives him. A psychiatrist would probably say it gives him an opportunity to safely work out his aggressiveness."

"And I suppose he's most aggressive where the blonde is concerned?" I asked sarcastically.

"If you weren't a stranger in town you'd have already heard some stories about that," Hazel said quietly. "Still, something's happened to that relationship lately." She frowned, a network of fine lines indenting her broad forehead. "I see it in her, not in him. She always had a cocky way of flipping a hip that had the pigeons crossing the street to bask in the sunlight. It used to be that when she snapped her fingers, Blaze rolled over. I don't see that now. She's lost weight. Her eyes look like two burnt holes in a blanket. Something's gnawing on her. I'll tell you the truth, I've been wondering if she isn't dipping into the till down there at the post office."

I had to hold myself down from sitting right up straight in the booth. "Why in the hell would she do that?"

Hazel planted both elbows firmly on the table top. "I'll tell you a tale out of school. When Charlie died, he left me some cash. I invested it. Then I wound up with this place. In a small town, that kind of thing gets magnified out of all proportion to the facts."

Her voice took on a brooding quality, as if she were thinking aloud. "Two months ago Blaze Franklin came to me and tried to borrow three thousand dollars. He had a red-hot business opportunity, he said. I'd learned from Charlie years ago how to keep an approach like that from being a problem. Blaze knew that my investments were managed for me by Nate Pepperman, a business consultant with an office up over the bank. I told Blaze to go and see Nate and explain his proposition, and that if Nate gave it his okay I said it was all right for Nate to milk something and finance the deal." Hazel gave me a little-girl grin. "I've seen Charlie send three a week like that to his 'business consultant,' and he'd light up another cigar and tell me that the day the guy okayed such a proposition was the day Charlie got himself a new business consultant. Most propositions when they couldn't lean on friendship turned out to be swiss cheese in texture."

She sobered again, placing her chin firmly in her cupped palms. "It must have been a couple of weeks later that Nate called me about something else, and I asked him about Blaze. I wasn't too much surprised to hear that Blaze had never been near him. A lot of the big-touch boys choke up in a hurry at the idea of trying to explain an if-and-when deal to a gimlet-eye like Nate."

She nudged a cigarette from the pack on the table and leaned forward to accept my proffered light. She blew out a lungful of smoke and licked at a filament of tobacco on her lip. "About the same time I heard from one of my customers that Lucille Grimes had been into his showroom pricing foreign sports cars. That seemed to be two and two adding up to four."

Hazel leveled the cigarette at me. "Then lo and behold, it seemed the very next time I saw Lucille she was burning up the rubber on a bright red, brand new MG roadster. I was curious enough about it to make it my business to find out Blaze had paid for it in cash. That's not the way the title reads, but that's what happened. So either old Blaze found himself a golden goose, after all, or Lucille is into the till and waitin' for her pants to be dropped and the paddle to burn her up. She sure looks it."

"Blaze probably saved up for it out of his green stamps," I said.

"For ten days or so Lucille was around everywhere in that car, champagne-bubbly," Hazel continued, unheeding. "Then the blight set in. I don't know what it was, or how he managed it, but the reins are very definitely in Mr. Franklin's hands these days. She looks like a lamp with the flame blown out. It must be that jealous men are hard on the nerves. She really looks like something was grindin' her down. Maybe a man wouldn't notice it, but it's there for a woman to see."

There was a lot that interested me in the story. A hell of a lot. Had I been knocking my brains out on the west coast of Florida's brush-grown back roads and here the two of them had been practically under my thumb all the time? Franklin's persistent interest in my timber-cruising, and then the connection to the post office—

I thought about it when the bar became busy and Hazel went back to it.

I thought about it some more on the way back to the motel.

I was already in bed when something else occurred to me. I got up and slipped into a robe and went outside to the Ford and opened the back deck lid and my big tool chest. I found what I was looking for, a miniature Italian automatic that fired three .17 cartridges. It had a little holster of its own that strapped on a man's shin.

I went back inside and strapped it on mine. I didn't know yet whether Manny Sebastian knew where to find me. When I found out, it could be on goddam short notice. I might need a little extra something like a hidden shin holster going for me.

But right now there was Blaze Franklin.

And Lucille Grimes.

I was in the post office lobby at nine o'clock in the morning. The outer doors were opened earlier to allow boxholders to get their mail, but the windows didn't open until nine. Right on the dot Lucille raised the General Delivery window. I could see two clerks behind her, but they were busy in the back end of the long room. I stepped up to the window, in a hurry to get my piece spoken before we were interrupted by someone walking in off the street. "Morning, Lucille," I said to her.

She looked surprised. "Good morning," she said almost as an afterthought. In the light of what Hazel had said I could see that Lucille was looking something less than her best. The deep, dark circles beneath her eyes were still in evidence, and the blonde hair looked less crisp. A trace of blotchiness marred the velvet pallor of her facial skin.

"May I help you?" she asked me.

"Depends, Lucille," I said with a breeziness I didn't feel. Some things I can do, but exchanging light badinage with a semistrange female isn't one of them. As a rule I leave that to the extroverts like Jed, but circumstances alter cases. "How about having dinner with me some one of these nights?"

Her original surprise was obviously redoubled. "I don't believe I should," she said. Having said it, she stood there testing the sound of it. "I really don't think—"

"You're not wearing his ring," I interrupted her. "Or his collar, I hope."

Her chin lifted. "If you're implying—"

"I'm implying I'd like to have dinner with you. Say Wednesday night?"

"I'll—let me think about it." She appeared confused.

A woman came in the door and walked up to the window. I had to step aside. "Wednesday night?" I pressed her as I did so.

"I'll have to—call me tonight," she said hurriedly, and smiled at the woman. "Yes, Mrs. Newman?"

I backed out tanglefootedly under Mrs. Newman's bright-eyed inspection. On the street I had to give only a very small plus to the operation. At least the blonde hadn't refused out of hand. For the moment I'd have to settle for that.

I walked across the street to where I'd parked the Ford and drove out east on Main. For six hours I beat my way up and back two dozen monstrously tangled dirt roads, logging trails, and footpaths, some of them no more than ten yards apart. I sweat gallons. I lost my temper. And I found nothing.

I went back to the Lazy Susan and showered and lay down on the bed for a couple of hours. The constant frustration was beginning to do things to the hair-trigger of my temper. I knew myself well enough to know that if it continued much longer some little shove from one direction or another would send me careening off on a course not necessarily the right one, just because action itself would be a release.

I was still in a bad mood when I whistled up Kaiser and headed out to the Dixie Pig for dinner. The first three minutes out there compounded it. I walked in to find Jed Raymond in the corner booth in the khaki shirt and red-piped gray trousers I'd come to associate with Blaze Franklin. It jarred me. "Where the hell's the masquerade?" I asked Jed. He looked up at me curiously. I didn't like the sound of my voice myself.

"I told you I was a jack-leg deputy in an emergency," he said cheerfully enough.

"So where's the emergency?"

His grin was sheepish. "Opening of a new supermarket." He ran a hand down the uniform. "I'm on traffic. I get called out a couple of times a month."

I sat down in the booth. "You must be younger than I thought. I don't see you somehow in this cops-and-robbers bit."

"Cut it out, will you?" Jed pleaded. "Around here a realtor is expected to either do this or go into politics. This takes less time and money."

"Suppose you had to arrest a real estate prospect, Jed?"

"Now you know no prospect of mine could ever be involved in anything requirin' me to arrest him," Jed replied with dignity.

"But suppose?"

"Suppose the moon is made of green cheese. Suppose the end of the world." Jed grinned. "If I hadn't got the deposit, though, he might have a little runnin' room."

Kaiser padded over to Jed's side of the booth and rested his muzzle on Jed's thigh. Jed reached down and scratched him between the ears, and Kaiser reached up and took Jed's arm in his mouth. Jed growled down at him, and Kaiser growled back. I could tell the dog wanted to play. Jed reached the same conclusion. "You want a little roughhouse, boy?" he inquired, and slid out of the booth and got down on his knees. In seconds the big gray-and-brown dog and Jed's ginger-colored crewcut were rolling all over the floor in a ferocious-sounding mock battle. It sounded so real the bar customers scattered like quail. One of them climbed up on a table.

Jed got to his feet finally, laughing, brushing the floor dirt from his uniform. Kaiser watched him with ears cocked alertly until Jed sat down in the booth again, then came back and sat down beside me. "That's a lot of dog," Jed said to me, and continued on in the same breath. "I heard you're dating Lucille Grimes."

"For chrissake, did she take an ad in the paper? She hasn't even said yes yet, for that matter."

"You broached your invitation in the hearing of a dear lady who can give a large-mouth bass cards and spades," Jed said drily.

I remembered the woman at the post office General Delivery window. "So, she still hasn't said yes."

"But you asked her." Jed held up a hand when I would have bitten off something short and snappy. "Hold it a minute, fire-eater. I feel a little guilt in the matter. Are you trying to prove something to me because I needled your semi-senior citizen status and threw you smack dab up against the shark-toothed widow?"

"Shark-toothed? What the hell are you talking about?"

"I live in this town, Chet. Do you need a blueprint?"

"For God's sake, I asked the woman to dinner. Does that leave me enlisted among her love-slaves?"

"It leaves you on Blaze Franklin's blacklist," Jed said soberly.

"How come Blaze Franklin's got this town buffaloed, Jed?"

He spread his hands. "You saw him. You sized him up."

"I sized him up," I agreed. "About twenty-five cents on the dollar."

"Goddammit, you're askin' for it with that attitude!" Jed bristled. "Hazel says Blaze came—"

"So Hazel knows about it, too. You sure *you* haven't taken an ad in the paper?"

Jed stared at me. "Aren't you a little touchy? I don't give a damn if you lay the blonde under the traffic light at high noon. I'm just concerned my big mouth pushed you into something with a stinger attached."

I pulled up on the reins. The kid meant all right. "All right, forget it, Jed. I asked her. She hasn't said yes or no. If she says yes we'll have dinner. If she says no we won't. It's a big deal?"

He folded his hands together on the table in front of him. "A couple of guys who've gone out with our beautiful postmistress have had—accidents. I don't believe she's had an invitation in a year. Until yours."

"How come no accidents happen to Franklin?"

"Maybe because he's got the town buffaloed. These weren't small accidents, Chet."

"I appreciate the concern, but it's premature, Jed. Can I buy you a drink before you go showing off that boy scout uniform?"

"I'll have to ask you to speak with more respect to this minion of th' law, suh. I'll take a raincheck on the drink." Jed rose to his feet, reached down to pat Kaiser on the head in passing, and went out the back door.

For the first time since I'd known the kid, I was glad to see him go. It's strange what the sight of a uniform does to me. On the other hand I was happy to see Kaiser take to him so quickly. If I had to pull stakes in a hurry, it meant I wouldn't be leaving the big dog high and dry.

I got up and walked over to the phone booth and looked up Lucille Grimes' home phone in the directory. There was no one near the booth when I dialed. "Chet Arnold, Lucille," I said when she answered. "How're we fixed for Wednesday night?"

"Oh, ah—" There was a five second pause. She hadn't repeated my name. I wondered if Franklin could possibly be right there with her. Not that I gave a damn. "Would five o'clock be too early? You could pick me up right at the post office."

"Five o'clock will be fine." So she didn't want me picking her up at her home for some reason. "See you then."

"I'm looking forward to it. Good night."

I replaced the receiver. She'd fairly cooed the last words. I felt a tingle at the base of my spine. Something about the way she'd said it—I don't know, I had a feeling. This attractively long-legged female wasn't saying yes only to dinner. Yet there was nothing soft about her. In Dixie Pig conversations I'd surprised an occasional feral gleam under the long-lashed lids. Unless I missed my guess she was a dandy little cutting tool.

Well, so much the better.

For some reason I've never been able to understand, I'm a much better man when I don't like them.

When I got back to the booth Hazel came over and sat down. "Jed coming back tonight after he gets off this deputy routine?" I asked her.

"Accordin' to him, he's goin' courtin'." She checked the bar with a sweeping glance before continuing. "That boy's goin' to make some girl a good husband time he makes up his mind to settle down."

"I wonder what it feels like," I said before I thought.

"You wonder what *what* feels like?"

"Oh, sitting with a girl on her living-room sofa." I tried to pass it off lightly. "Object: matrimony, if you can't get it any other way."

"You never tried it? No, I s'pose not," she answered her own question. She didn't pursue aloud her chain of thought. A silence settled down between us.

"I've been thinking—" I began, finally.

"Do you suppose—" Hazel started in the same breath.

We both laughed, and she waved a hand. "You've got the floor, horseman."

I couldn't seem to find the right words. "Maybe we ought to try it again some night," I said at last.

She didn't reply for a moment. "There's a point to it?" she asked when I'd begun to think she wasn't going to answer at all.

"There could be. You've made a losing bet or two in your day, haven't you?"

"I wish they'd only been cash." She sounded quite sober. "Why do you want to try it again, Chet?"

"Maybe because the next time I came in here after the other night you didn't have 'Chet Arnold is an impotent slob' up on the front in neon lights."

"What the hell do you think I am?" she began indignantly, and then started to laugh. "Can that corn, man. Why do you?"

"It offends my miserly soul to see such a stack of material going to waste."

"I suppose even a left-handed compliment is more than I rate most days around here," she said good-humoredly. "All right, I'll stop fishing." She reached across the table and covered my hand with hers just for a second before removing it again. "And listen, man: the fact you want to is what counts with me. I've been around gamblers long enough to know that a lot of the time they're wired into different sockets." She rose briskly as a glass bottom rapped on the bar. "I'll be back."

I watched her walk away from me back to the bar, and all of a sudden I knew it was going to be all right. I never know how I know, the times I do. I just know.

I waited for her to come back, but the bar stayed busy. I got up finally and walked over to one end of it, away from the customers. "I'll be back at lock-up time," I told Hazel when she came down the bar toward me.

Her eyes widened. I think she started a wisecrack but choked it off. "I'll be ready," was all she said.

I drove downtown. I had a couple of hours to kill, and I might as well kill them at Bobby Herman's place. I left Kaiser in the car and went on into the tavern. Herman was friendly with me now, mostly because I let him show off his encyclopedic baseball knowledge by asking him trick questions only a buff could know the answers to. Bobby had never seen a major league game in his life, except in spring training, but he read *The Sporting News* religiously, and he remembered what he read. He had the type of mind that could rattle off the batting order lineups for the Yankees and the Pirates in the '28 World Series. I remembered that series myself. That had been the year I'd been expelled from school for stalking the fat boy whose boxer dog had killed Fatima.

Herman's place drew a workingman crowd. He stayed open till midnight, but on week-nights his customers generally packed it in around ten. The last hour he always had time to talk, and over the last three weeks I'd made it my business to see to it that a lot of his talking was done to me.

I was later than usual tonight. There was only one other customer at the bar when I sat down there, and a boy and a girl in the farthest booth. Bobby whisked his bar rag over the mahogany in front of me and slapped down a tight-collared beer. "Big argument in here tonight," he informed me. "You remember the year Cobb an' Speaker wound up playin' the outfield for the Philadelphia Athletics when they were through in Detroit and Cleveland? Well, the argument was who was the third man in that outfield. I say it was Fothergill. Some of the guys say it was Heilmann. Who do you think it was?"

"If you say Fothergill, I'll settle for Fothergill, Bobby," I told him. He grinned, pleased, and retreated to his wash rack and started rinsing out glasses. The only other customer at the bar finished his beer, grunted goodnight, and went out the door. The only sound in the place was the low murmur of voices from the corner booth and the clink of glasses as Bobby placed them on the drainboard. When he looked up my way again I was ready for him. I nodded down the bar in a way that took in two thirds of the tavern. "Say, whatever happened to the big dark guy used to stand down there when I first started coming in? Big, rugged-looking guy."

Bobby paused with a sparkling glass in his hand. He frowned, trying to think. "Big, rugged—? Oh, yeah. The one with the scar on his throat. That's right, I haven't seen him lately. Must've found greener pastures. He wasn't a regular, anyway."

I felt a tight sensation in the pit of my stomach. "He work around here? He reminded me of someone, and I finally remembered who it was. I thought I'd ask him if he was related."

Herman had returned to his glasses. "I don't know if he works around here. He's not a native, though. Real quiet fella. Drove a blue sedan with out-of-state plates. Probably a tourist."

A real quiet fella. Even after seeing it so many times it always surprised me the way the mute Bunny could walk into a bar, get his first beer by holding up a finger as the bartender drew one for someone else, and all the refills he wanted by snapping a coin down on the bar. He never joined a group but always stood just in the background, smiling and nodding at the general conversation. He had a trick of anticipating a direct question and turning his shoulder so that his attention appeared to be elsewhere and the question flew harmlessly over it. I've seen people lose hard cash betting Bunny could talk after they'd been around him for days.

"Could he be staying up at the Walton House? Seems to me I saw a blue sedan parked up there."

"Don't think so." Bobby dried his hands on his apron front. "Every time I saw him pull out of the lot here he'd swing it around and head out east from the traffic light." He paused as if checking his memory. "I don't think he lived in town."

"Oh, well, it's not that important," I said. I looked at my watch. "Put one more head on this thing, anyway, Bobby. Then maybe your sterling salesmanship can get me to exceed my quota."

I started Herman off on baseball again along with my second beer. He rattled along, happy with the sound of his own voice. I had only to contribute an occasional nod. His confident statistics bounced off me as I sat there thinking about Bunny.

It was a comfort to know I'd been right in my guess that Bunny had hidden out east on Main as I'd originally figured. I'd been beginning to wonder. I might be stubborn, but I had no intention of working my way through to the east coast of Florida a side road at a time. With Herman's memory to strengthen my first guess, though, I'd just have to keep at it. Bunny was out there, somewhere. I had no illusions, of course, that I was going to be able to do him any good.

I was out in the back parking lot when Hazel came out at ten after twelve. She had a dress on again. I walked around the Ford to open the door for her, and she loomed up over me a good four inches. I got a whiff of an exotic perfume as she climbed into the car.

"Relax," I told her as I headed down the driveway. "Everything's going to be all right."

"I just hope you're not building yourself up for a letdown," she said doubtfully.

"It's all right," I repeated.

I drove with my left hand and we held hands, her left in my right. The full moon was past and it was a much darker night. I nearly missed the turn-off road completely. I had to back up for it. We jolted down the final rutted three hundred yards, and sat looking at the cabin that was just a darker blotch in the blackness.

On the porch Hazel gave me her key and I opened the door. It was so quiet it hurt the ears. My pulse must have been doing a hundred and seventy. We didn't bother with any lights. Hand-in-hand we stumbled through the doorway from the living room into the bedroom beyond.

I undressed her myself. With each layer removed she showed up whiter and whiter, until she gleamed in the dark like the phosphoresence in the gulf. I didn't bother with her cowboy boots. She still had them on when we settled down on the bed. She wasn't making a sound. I could hear the click of the boot heels when her legs came together over my back. I went for broke, and made it. Made it so big it was one lumped-up soul-satisfying taste deep in my throat. I could feel the wild pulse in her neck under my lips. When she got excited herself it was a damn good thing for me there were no spurs on the boots.

I don't know how long it was before she spoke. I could still hear her heavy breathing—or was it mine?—and her voice was a deeply muted, husky sound. "Welcome back, horseman. For an off-again, on-again, Finnegan type you cover a spread of ground."

I didn't say anything. I slid my hands beneath her and took a solid double-handful of her powerful buttocks. I pulled her up against me again, tightly.

"Oh, no!" she chuckled. "Honest to Christmas, Chet—" She started to laugh, a full-throated richness of sound that remained in my mind long after it had died out in my ears.

It was the finest sound I'd heard in longer than I liked to think about.

I was on my back, relaxed, smoking a cigarette when Hazel came back into the bedroom and sat down on the edge of the bed. She reached over to punch me on the arm. "You ride a mean rodeo, horseman," she said to me. "An' here you had me thinkin' there was no fire in the boiler at all." I could feel her bending over me, trying to find my face in the dark.

"There's fire enough baby, when the damn engineer's on the job." I threw away the cigarette, remembered too late the wooden cabin, and got up and found a shoe and ground out the cigarette with the heel. I came back to the bed. "Trouble is every so often he takes these two-week lunch hours."

Her big arms reached up and pulled me down beside her. "The hell with it. At the moment I couldn't care less." She stretched beside me, lengthily. A healthy animal. "Although I'll admit I don't understand it."

I understood it. Up to a point, anyway. I was just geared to a different ratio. With me it just wasn't the main line the way it was with most guys. It never had been, and I'd never had any reason to think it ever would be. Although with this big, warm-hearted, two-hundred-percent woman—

She stirred beside me. "Funny how all right it can make things, huh? When it's right?"

"You said a hammered-down mouthful, baby."

Her voice was softer when she spoke again. "Nobody's ever called me 'baby'. It sounds—nice."

I reached for her in the dark. "Turn around here and let me play with the best part of you."

"Oh, well, look, now. Let's not overdo this thing, pardner."

She sounded really worried. I laughed out loud. "You sound like the bride who saw her husband dressing after their wedding night and burst into tears. 'I liked it s-so much,' she sobbed, 'and we've used up s-so much of it!'"

Hazel batted me. I grabbed to find and hold her hard-punching hands. It was remarkable the unanimity with which our intentions changed at the same instant.

I don't know what time it was when we got out of there. The dressing had been interrupted a couple of times. The shower had run, and stopped, and run, and stopped, and run, and stopped. The bathroom looked as if a couple of whales had been turned loose. There was water even on the ceiling.

Hazel came in, dressed, while I was conducting a mopping-up operation with towels. "Leave it," she said. "I'll drive out tomorrow and take care of it."

We rode back to the Dixie Pig in a comfortable silence. I put her in her car. She ran down her window and waved to me before she drove off.

I set sail for the motel, and bed.

I woke with a start from my first deep sleep. A glance at the luminous dial on the alarm clock beside the bed indicated I'd been asleep thirty minutes. From somewhere my subconscious had put together a neat, tight little package: kick the whole bit in Hudson, and take off with Hazel. For anywhere. Catch up on living for a change.

I looked around the motel room's long, dappled shadows and mottled dark corners. I listened to the thump as some-one turned over in bed in the next room, plainly audible through the thin partition.

I didn't even need the cold light of day to squelch that crazy idea.

Don't be a bigger goddam fool than nature intended, I told myself.

I knew what I was.

At my age no leopard changes his spots.

I closed my eyes again.

After awhile I even slept.

I picked Lucille up on the dot of five in front of the post office. "Since it's early enough for a drive, I made a reservation at the Black Angus," I said. "Okay?"

"It's a very nice place," she said in reply. She smoothed her skirt out beneath her, palms flat against the pliant thighs. Her eyes were bright, and her nostrils flared. There was something between us from the second she stepped into the Ford.

I headed north on the highway and just rolled it along. It was about a thirty mile drive. Without being obvious about it, I watched the rear-view mirror. I saw no indication of a jealous man in pursuit, but Jed's warning was on my mind.

We didn't exchange fifteen words on the way. She sat beside me in seeming lassitude. I was satisfied to leave it that way for the time being. I thought I'd have a chance over dinner to probe a little bit and see what it was that made this woman tick.

It didn't work out that way. In the huge dining room she had three cocktails in quick succession. She apologized for the third, but downed it quicker than the other two. I ordered a good meal, but she just toyed with her food. Conversation remained at a mininum. She closed out my tentative leads with terse replies, her tone brittle. Her responses featured incomplete sentences, dangling phrases, and half-finished expressions, punctuated by an occasional dazzling, loose-lipped smile. An aura of almost febrile excitement emanated from her. I almost expected to see sparks fly from her fingers and toes. She was the epitome of promise.

I suggested brandy afterward. She settled for a highball. She had two, then another. She took on a high gloss. She pronounced her words carefully. Leaving, she stepped a little bit too high over the threshold.

In the car she lapsed into complete silence. Her eyes were fixed dreamly straight ahead down the road. If she felt the car slow down as I studied the motels we came up to, she gave no sign. When she did speak, she surprised me. "This one," she said huskily, and pointed. I turned down a long driveway that wound between individual cabins set back from the edge of the road. I stopped at the one marked "Office" and got out and went inside. Lucille stayed in the car.

I registered under the bored eye of the bald-headed manager. With practiced ease he read my "Mr. and Mrs. Chet Arnold" upside down. "Anything special, Mr. Arnold?"

"A quiet one."

"Certainly, sir." He turned to the key-rack behind him.

When he faced front again, I was filling in another card. "That one's for my brother-in-law and his wife," I said, pointing to the Arnold card. "I'll pay you for both."

The manager dropped the key in his hand on the Arnold card and turned to get another. Again he performed his upside-down reading stunt on the second card. "This one's every bit as good, Mr. Reynolds. They're together, the last two on the right."

"Fine." I paid him, picked up both keys, and went out to the car. The keys were numbers 10 and 11. Number 10 was the Arnolds' cabin. Number 11 was the Reynolds'. I drove to the end of the wooded lot and stopped in front of number 11. I got out and let Lucille out on her side, opened the cabin door, and stepped aside to let her enter. "Back in a second," I told her.

I went back to the Ford and backed it off the driveway and around on the grass behind the cabin. I parked it between two trees. We'd eaten so early the sky was still bright overhead, but under the trees it was nearly dark.

Lucille displayed no curiosity about my short trip. She had every light in the place on when I got back inside. She was humming to herself, and moving slowly about the room in a way that suggested a dance step. Her eyes were the biggest part of her face. Without saying a word she began to undress, leisurely.

I went into the bathroom and closed the door. I took off my jacket and my shoulder holster. I removed the Smith & Wesson from the holster and a towel from the rack, and I wrapped the gun loosely in the towel. I put the holster in a jacket pocket, put the jacket back on, and went out, carrying the towel.

Lucille was sitting on the edge of the bed in her panties. She smiled up at me lazily. The tip of her tongue flicked over her lips. I put the towel down carefully on the small night table, and sat down on the bed beside her. I stood her up, between my feet, and made a production of removing the panties. Her thighs were tanned, her buttocks milky. She looked like a two-toned animal.

She crawled onto the bed and lay there face down while I stood up and undressed. I left my shoes on. I walked to the door and locked and bolted it. When I turned, she had rolled part-way over, watching me. Her eyes looked almost filmed. Her head was up an inch or two from the pillow, slightly turned, as though she were listening.

I was listening, too.

I walked back to her. I was only a stride from the bed when we both heard it with no trouble at all. There was a splintering crash from next door as the door of number 10 went down. I could hear the thump of heavy boots as Blaze Franklin blundered around in the dark in the next cabin, looking for the light.

Lucille's eyes widened as she realized I'd somehow sucked him into the wrong cabin. Her breasts bobbed as she filled her lungs to scream. I reached down and slapped her squarely in her bare belly. She got out a gargle. That's all.

I knew Franklin couldn't stay to hunt for us. The Smith & Wesson and my shoes were just insurance against his being smarter than I thought he was. Right now he was all done on this caper. He had no business there. He had to get away from the empty cabin he'd broken into. Not seeing the Ford, he had to think we'd come and gone already.

I covered Lucille's mouth with my hand till I heard the whine of the cruiser pulling away. Even in the dirt the tires sang. I took my hand off her face. It was no blacker under the trees outside than in the depths of her eyes. "You get a bang out of watching him beat them up?" I asked her.

Her mouth was wet. "He makes them crawl," she said almost in a whisper. She didn't look particularly afraid. "What are you going to do?"

"I'll show you what I'm going to do." I took hold of her. She may not have been the best I'd ever had in my hands, but she was a useful piece of machinery. She submitted passively until she realized my intention. She fought hard, then. She was strong, but not strong enough. She hissed like a cat all the time I abused her.

It was four in the morning before we left there.

Fifty per cent of us had enjoyed it.

I drove back to Hudson and let Lucille out up the street from her house. False dawn was lightening the sky. I didn't want to drive right up to her door in case Franklin was waiting for her on her front porch.

She hadn't said a word all the way back to town. She looked around when I stopped the car. It took her a moment to recognize where she was. She opened the car door and got out, then leaned back in to spit at me. "Blaze will kill you for this," she rasped.

I appreciate a good hater. "You've got it all wrong, sugar," I told her. "You're going to have a hard time explaining this to your jealous lord and master. You set up the place, and then you weren't there. What does Blaze use on *you* when he's a little out of sorts? His belt? A jealous man believes what he wants to believe. Blaze is going to figure you as a partner in the disappearance."

I could have counted to ten while she stared in at me. I'd given her something to think about. Without another word she slammed the door and started up the street. She was unsteady on her high heels. I sat and watched her go.

It wasn't hard to see where Jed Raymond had found the adjective "shark-toothed" in connection with the widow Grimes. I owed the kid something for keeping me from making the play with my eyes shut. Franklin and the blonde must have had a Roman holiday with the suitors she'd set up for the deputy to knock over. And of course none of them would talk.

I couldn't show much of a plus on the real purpose of the evening. There hadn't been much of the conversation I'd counted on. On the other hand, it had done me good to vent some poison on a truly poisonous female.

I started the Ford up, and eased through the deserted square in the direction of the Lazy Susan. I parked a block away and came up on it from the rear. I thought I had

Franklin figured, but until I knew for sure I had to be ready to see him on short notice. There was no cruiser in the motel yard. I walked completely around it, my feet silent on the grass. Through the office window I could see the night clerk with his head nodding. There was no sign at all of Franklin. Lucille would be lucky if it was tomorrow instead of right now that she was down on her knees trying to explain.

I went into my unit and showered and shaved. It was full dawn when I stretched out on the bed.

I was beginning to get a feeling about Lucille Grimes and Blaze Franklin.

I had to figure out a way of getting at them.

I interrupted Hazel in her preoccupied feeding of potato chips to Kaiser in our booth at the Dixie Pig. "That's the third time in ten minutes you've given me the double-O inspection as if you were looking for ringworm. What gives?"

"Just looking for battle wounds. I heard you had a date with the blonde last night."

"This *is* a small town. You've got her all wrong, though. She's really quite kittenish."

Hazel snorted. "So's a Rocky Mountain panther. I don't get it. Can it be that the light in your baby blues has re-formed her?"

"How did she get into the conversation, anyway?" I evaded Hazel. "Let's get to something important, like what's on your schedule after closing tonight."

"I could run out in back and check my social calendar, but I'll take a chance and say I'm free." She smiled, a warm, golden smile. "Did you have a discussion period in mind, horseman?"

"If you can discuss on your back."

"My, my, what a rejuvenation." She knuckled a big hand and pushed gently at mine on the table. The smile on her lips overflowed to her eyes. "Who was the best sprinter you ever saw at four furlongs?"

"I'd have to make it a dead-heat among Decathlon, White Skies, and Moolah Bux, I guess."

"Bet you I could give the field a length start an' beat them to the back door tonight." Hazel rose to her feet. "Let me get out of here before I entirely lose my maidenly reserve," she said briskly. She wagged a finger at me. "You watch out for that woman, y'hear? She's tricky."

"And here I thought I'd changed the subject."

Hazel smiled again, and went back to the bar. I took over her job of feeding potato chips to Kaiser. The big dog was gone for potato chips. I'd tested him with a potato chip versus a piece of steak. He ate the steak, but he ate the potato chip first. He'd crunch a chip, and then circle his muzzle with his tongue to get all the salt.

This town had already given me one surprise in the appearance of the red-headed Eddie from Manny Sebastian's parking lot. When I looked up toward the rear entrance of the Dixie Pig between potato chips, I had a second. Lucille Grimes was halfway across the floor heading toward my booth.

Her hands were empty. Her bag dangled loosely from the strap on her arm. That much I took in in the first split second. Then she was standing beside the booth. "Sit down, if you can," I greeted her. "What color welts are you wearing these days?"

She attempted a smile, but her eyes were murderous. She sat down. I watched carefully until she laid her bag aside. I had no intention of playing clay pigeon for this dolly. From the second she started talking it was plain she had herself under a tight rein. "I came by to ask you to dinner tomorrow night."

Now here was a switch. "Yeah? Where?"

"At my house."

Come into my parlor, said the spider to the fly. "At your house? What's the occasion?"

"I want to talk to you." Even she seemed to realize that was a little weak. "I might have a proposition for you."

"What about?"

She manufactured a smile. "Why don't you come and see? Possibly I can use someone as foresighted as you appear to be."

"In the post office?"

She stood up. "Call me in the morning and let me know." She picked up her bag and walked to the door. Her movements weren't as fluid as I remembered them.

I moved out of the corner of the booth away from the

window when she went out the door. This was no campfire girl. The dinner invitation had to mean one of two things. Either Franklin was so crazy mad to get at me he was willing to drop a ton on me right in her house, or Franklin had given her such a hard way to go the blonde was looking for reinforcements to get her out from under Franklin. I couldn't see much nourishment for me in either setup.

Of course if it was Franklin and the blonde who actually had short-circuited Bunny—

I decided I'd have to give the invitation more thought.

Out at the cabin I walked from the bathroom into the bedroom and looked down at Hazel tastefully attired in one thirty-second of a sheet. "Come on and let's take a shower, big stuff," I said.

She yawned, and stretched mightily. The effect was spectacular. "You must have otter blood in you, man," she complained drowsily. "The last two nights with you I been in an' out of that shower till my corns are waterlogged. Why don't you just tumble on down here an' relax your—"

As close as we'd been recently it had remained no secret that Hazel was touchy. I leaned down and goosed her, and she bounded from the bed to the middle of the room with a strangled yelp. I aimed my thumb at her again, and she flew into the bathroom. I herded her into the glassed-in compartment and turned on the fine needle-spray. I adjusted it to warm, and stepped in with her. We each took soap and in silence began to lather each other.

The water hissed softly, the single off-center fluorescent light glistened dimly upon sleek flesh, and warm hands glided gently over slippery body contours. It was a moment out of a lifetime. We stayed in the shower a long time.

The place was just about afloat when I stepped out and grabbed a towel. I picked up another one and handed it to Hazel, still in the shower. She turned the water off and buried her wet red head in the towel. I reached in behind her and flipped the handle over to full cold.

"Ooooooh-h-h!" I never heard such a catamount yowl in my life. Hazel boomed out of the shower like a fullback. She ran right over me. I was laughing so hard that when she turned and came after me, I couldn't defend myself.

She got me down and enthusiastically banged my head on the tile. I couldn't get her off till I got into her ribs and tickled. She squealed, and rolled away.

Several wet towels and a couple of cigarettes later we were stretched out on the bed, the firefly glow of cigarettes the bedroom's only light. Beside me I could hear Hazel's deep, even breathing. She reached up over me to stub out her cigarette in the ashtray on the table beside the bed, and trailed her hand lightly along my body as she dropped back with a sigh. "You don't happen to think you're pretty far out sometimes reaching for sensations, horseman?" she asked in her rich voice.

"You can tell your grandchildren someday you did it under water," I told her.

She laughed, then sobered. "That parlay breaks down with the first dog out of the box. Children come before grandchildren, unless they've repealed a law of nature."

I didn't like what I heard in her voice. I changed the subject. "I didn't get a chance to tell you before, but I'm invited out to dinner tomorrow night."

Hazel came up on an elbow. "The blonde?"

"In the solid flesh."

In the increased glow of my cigarette as I took a final drag I could see the outline of her features, but not her expression. "Chet," she began, and hesitated. She seemed to be wondering whether to continue. "I don't want to know your business, Chet, and I'm not jealous of Lucille Grimes, but there's something I think you ought to know." She stopped again. I could have made it easier for her, but I didn't. I didn't because jealous was exactly what I thought she was. She made me sorry right away. "Blaze Franklin is asking questions about you all over town, Chet."

Instinct is a wonderful thing. I didn't have a stitch on, but my hand was up reaching for the butt of the Smith & Wesson in the shoulder holster with my clothes in the next room. "Like what kind of questions is he asking?"

"Where you came from. What you're doing here. Where you lived before. How much talking you do about yourself." Hazel's tone was quiet. "I don't want you to think I'm prying, Chet. I just thought you ought to know."

"Don't think I don't appreciate it." I thought about Blaze

Franklin. It looked as though I had indeed underestimated the gentleman. He wasn't asking those particular questions because of anything that had happened between Lucille and me. I had no damn business lying here bed-bouncing with the wash out on the line and a storm coming up. "Any reaction from the questioned?" I asked Hazel.

"Even Jed was saying it was odd how little we really knew about you." There was no emphasis in the remark. She was reporting a fact. Her hand came up and settled on my arm. "I'm going to say one more thing, and then I'm going to shut up. If you think of anything I can do to help, let me know." She rolled over and sat up on the edge of the bed. "Let's get dressed," she said briskly. "I'm a workin' gal, and I've got to open up in the morning."

It was a fact the life had gone out of the party. We dressed and locked up and went out to the Ford. On the way back to town I had time to think about Hazel's last remark. "'If you think of anything I can do to help, let me know.'" That was just short of putting it in writing that she was on the team. More than that, she didn't care what the name on the uniform was. In my life I've run into few blanket endorsements. The big woman was all gold and a yard wide.

I appreciated it, as I'd told her, but I was damn well going to put a stop to it. She could get nothing but hurt.

It was two thirty when I turned into the Dixie Pig's crushed stone driveway and let her out beside her car. The routine good nights were an anticlimax.

I drove to the motel. There was only one reason Franklin could be asking those questions about me. He was interested in my interest in the saw-grass swamps and savanna intermingled with pine-land, salt meadows, and mangrove thickets on the east side of town. Franklin had stamped the brand on himself. Franklin was the reason I had come to Hudson.

Granting the fact, it left unanswered questions. How had a mule-head like Franklin outmaneuvered Bunny? Bunny could break him up with his bare hands. And why was Franklin nosing around me when by all rights he should have been lying doggo hoping nobody was looking in his direction?

I didn't know.

I didn't know, but I knew I was going to start finding out at dinner with Lucille Grimes.

There was no question now about my accepting that unwilling invitation.

For two thirds of its length the dinner was an eighteen-karat flop. We sat at opposite ends of a six foot table, and were served by a kid in a maid's uniform. Lucille sat at her end with an expression like an aristocrat among the peasantry. All I could think of was Lady Bountiful among the poor.

It was obvious that with the lady at the head of the table I was a stink in the nostrils. It was interesting that feeling as she did about me, Franklin had been able to force her into issuing this dinner invitation. It made Hazel a hundred per cent right about who was wearing the pants in the corporation.

Franklin was pushing her to set up the deadfall again. He didn't know what had happened to her that night. She wouldn't tell him. Franklin would naturally assume that after this expression of her majesty's gracious favor I would press hard for another date. Lucille knew better, but she had to go along with the idea.

It gave me an idea of my own.

"Glad to see you finally wised up to Franklin," I said to her when the little maid disappeared after serving the dessert.

Lucille's mind had been a long way off. Probably gloating over a mental image of me staked out over an anthill. She came back to earth in a hurry. "Wised up?"

"Sure. What the hell you ever saw in a jerk like that I'll never know. A big bag of wind." It was no trouble to make that sound convincing. "Having me to dinner like this shows you're a smart girl. You should have cut him loose a long time ago. You and I, now—we could really play chopsticks together on the same piano."

She didn't swallow it hook, line and sinker. Not at first. Her eyes were suspicious as I oiled up both sides of my tongue and greased her liberally. She couldn't believe at first I was so stupid as not to know her reaction to me, but the suspicion gradually died. She was used to such a response, for one thing. By the end of the meal she'd come as alive as though someone had just reported my painful demise. She was tossing them back to me as fast as I batted them at her.

Lucille was no fool. I was giving her an out on a problem on which she hadn't been able to see daylight. As far as Franklin was concerned, this was the way it was supposed to go. If she could report progress to him, that was a load off her back. If she could report progress that turned out to be fact, and that put my neck under the knife, why how lovely. She had nothing to lose.

She didn't overplay her hand a bit, either. "I was very angry with you the other evening," she said gravely. "I thought you were a gentleman."

Even the boob that I was supposed to be couldn't let her get away with that one. "You'd just set me up to get cut off at the knees, sweetheart. You're lucky I didn't really get mad at you."

"But you know I wasn't going to do anything—I wasn't—"

"You were just going to sit there and cheer. You got what was coming to you. Just like Franklin's going to one of these days." I threw that in as an afterthought. If she were really getting restless under the Franklin thumb—

She didn't appear to notice the opening. Honest curiosity shone for an instant through the genteel facade. "I admire clever men. Whatever led you to take rooms in two different names?"

"Self-preservation. I was at the head of the line when it was passed around. Look, maybe I was too rough with you, but admit it, you had it coming. I don't see why that means we can't get along. You're a smart girl. You and I make a much better team than you and Franklin. Just don't you try any more cute tricks and we'll be all right. I don't like bossy women. Do as you're told and we'll have no trouble."

I almost expected to hear her grinding her teeth after that little speech, but she smiled sweetly. She was a cinch to bring along a sawed-off baseball bat herself to our next motel room assignation. It oozed out of every ounce of her without her realizing it that she just couldn't wait to drag down into the dust the nose of this loud-mouthed braggart who had abused her. "I'll admit I'm not used to such a—

such a forceful man," she said. "Shall we have our coffee on the patio?"

We had our coffee on the patio. I buttered her up some more. She buttered me up some more. Instead of the silver fingerbowls that were placed on our trays twin shower-baths would have been more appropriate.

She finally cut across the radius of the circle to the hub of the wheel. "What are you really doing in this area?" she asked me directly. "I never have believed that black maple story."

"A man can make a quick dollar if he stumbles onto the right patch of second growth out in that timber," I argued.

She wasn't ready now to let me get away with it. "You don't seem to me like the type of man interested in making a few dollars at a time."

I drained off the rest of my coffee and set my cup down with a gesture of finality. I rose to my feet. She rose, too, surprised. "You talk too much, sweetheart," I told her. I walked around the little marble table and took her by the arms, just below the edges of her short-sleeved dress, harder than I needed to. "You're going to have to break that habit." I shook her gently to and fro, not hard, but her face whitened at the pressure on her arms. "I'll give you a chance starting tomorrow night at dinner. Pick you up at five?"

"I'll—all right. Five," she said breathlessly.

"Okay." I let her go. Her hands came up instinctively to caress her arms. My handprints stood out on them lividly. "Thanks for the dinner. See you at five tomorrow. Good night."

"Good night," she echoed numbly.

I went down the outside walk to the street without going back through the house. I would have given a dollar bill to know what she was thinking as she stood there and watched me go. But on second thought I realized it would have been a dollar wasted.

She'd see to it that Franklin took me tomorrow night.

So she thought.

I'd see to it I took the pair of them.

I was positive now. Tomorrow night I'd wind up the whole ball of yarn.

I drove back to the motel and parked in the yard. It was

still early, but I didn't feel like going out to the Dixie Pig. I opened the motel unit door carefully because Kaiser had a habit of sleeping against it. He wasn't against it this time. He was sprawled in the left-hand corner with his head at an awkward angle.

"Close the door," a voice said from behind it. Manny Sebastian's fat figure stepped into view. His hands were empty. The hands of the sandy-haired, bucktoothed man who moved out beside him weren't empty. A blued-steel revolver was trained steadily on my chest.

I stepped inside and closed the door.

Bucktooth moved to my right, the gun steady. "Don't get careless," he said. His eyes were red-rimmed and wild-looking. I could see him only from the corner of my eye as his free hand snaked under my jacket and delicately removed the Smith & Wesson from its holster. He tossed it to Manny.

"He carries a Colt, too," Manny said. His round, swarthy face was shiny with perspiration.

From behind me Bucktooth gave me the shoulders-to-knees hand-patting treatment. He discovered the Woodsman in my pants pocket. He didn't make the mistake of trying to take it out himself. "Throw it on the bed," he ordered me. "And be goddam careful how you do it."

I fished the .22 out with thumb and forefinger, and tossed it at the bed. I could see Manny relax. I wondered how the bastards would feel if they knew I still had the little three-shot .17 caliber puff adder on my shin.

"Let's get out of here," Bucktooth said from behind me.

"We're going to take a little ride," Manny informed me. He was mopping at his streaming features with a soggy handkerchief. My Smith & Wesson was in his other hand.

I went over and knelt down beside Kaiser. He was still breathing. There was a ragged, bleeding furrow on his head between his ears, right alongside the still half-healed one from his trip into the ditch. I stood up and turned around. Bucktooth had moved in only six feet away from me, his gun reversed in his hand, the butt exposed. "Did you hit the dog, you sonofabitch?" I asked him.

"Just like I'll belt you if you make one more move like that without being told," he snarled.

I walked into him, swinging.

"Don't shoot! Don't shoot!" Manny bleated from behind me. "He's got to talk first!"

Bucktooth stepped back far enough so I missed him with my first swing. He stepped right back in again and clubbed at me with the gun. I got my head out of the way, but he landed on my left shoulder the same instant I smashed my right hand into his belly. I was staggering sideways when he doubled up. Before I could catch my balance Manny clocked me on the back of the neck with my own gun. I was on my knees all of a sudden without realizing how I'd got there. The room whirled sickeningly.

"Cut it out!" Manny said sharply to Bucktooth, who was lunging at me with upraised gun. Manny stepped in between us. "You can have your fun later." Bucktooth hesitated, his red eyes slitted. Reluctantly he backed away. "Get up," Manny said to me. I got to my feet, wobbly. "Where's the stuff?"

"Fifteen, eighteen miles out in the swamp," I mumbled.

"Didn't I tell you he'd say that?" Bucktooth growled.

"And didn't I tell you it didn't matter what he said?" Manny rebutted. "If it isn't wherever he takes us to, then you exercise that gun butt." He waved the Smith & Wesson at me. "Let's get going."

"Can't find th' tree—at night," I said.

"I don't expect to. We'll go in the morning. Right now we'll go to our place. Less chance of an interruption."

"The dog goes with us," I told him.

"Now here's one practicin' to be a character," Bucktooth said in a wondering tone. He shoved his face into mine. "The dog goes nowhere, jerk!"

"I'll show you where to leave him," I said.

Bucktooth made a sound deep in his throat. Manny caught his arm as he started to swing it. "We can't leave the dog here looking like that in an empty room," he said. He looked at me. "What's your play?"

"I know someone who'll take care of him," I answered. "Open the door. I'll carry him."

"No!" Bucktooth said violently.

"Pick him up," Manny said to me. "The dog will make a good excuse if we run onto anyone," he shut off his angry partner. "Shut up, will you? Rudy Hernandez told me years ago the guy was like this about animals."

I picked up Kaiser. In the shape I was in it was a hell of a lift. Bucktooth was right beside me. "Pretty soon I'm gonna ask you what happened to Red, pal," he said softly. "Right now you make one wrong move or one bit of noise an' you've had it. I won't kill you, but you'll wish I had. I'll break every bone in your stupid face."

"Open the door," I said.

Instead he leveled the gun at me again. "I'll cover you from the doorway till you get him in the car," he told Manny.

Manny opened the door. It was black night outside. I carried Kaiser out. Manny pointed to a big station wagon parked on the rim of the driveway. He opened the front door on the passenger's side. There wasn't a soul around. I climbed into the front seat with Kaiser on my lap. Manny got under the wheel. In seconds I could hear Bucktooth crawling into the seat behind me. I don't know if I could feel or sense his gun three-quarters of an inch from the short hairs at the back of my neck.

Manny took the wagon out of there. I'd intended to take Kaiser to the Dixie Pig, but rolling through town I saw a light on in Jed Raymond's second floor office. "Pull in anywhere here," I said. Bucktooth's gun came up level with my head as the car swung into the curb.

"What's the play?" Manny said to me again.

"See that light up there? I'll carry the dog up one flight of stairs and leave him outside the door of the real estate office."

"And I suppose you'll okay that, too," Bucktooth rasped at Manny.

"I'd just as soon humor him till we get our hands on the stuff," Manny said defensively. "This is one stubborn sonofabitch."

"I'll unstubborn him or anyone else in three an' a half

minutes, guaranteed," Bucktooth snapped, but he opened his door and got out. He opened my door. "Come on, you. Sometimes I think the whole damn world's crazy."

I lugged Kaiser up the stairs and laid him down gently outside Jed's door. Bucktooth stayed a yard behind me all the way. I knew that if Kaiser came to before Jed found him, the big dog would smell Jed inside and wouldn't leave.

We were back in the wagon in two minutes. I felt a lot better. Jed would take care of Kaiser. I knew Kaiser liked him. Now I could concentrate on getting rid of these mongolian idiots.

Manny headed north on U.S. 19. About two miles above town he turned into a second-rate motel. "No noise," Bucktooth warned me as we got out of the wagon. By way of emphasis he banged me viciously in the ribs with his gun butt when Manny's back was turned. I nearly went down. Stumbling inside the motel room, I began to make plans for Bucktooth.

With the door closed, Manny turned to me. "How do we get to the stuff?"

"Airboat," I said.

Manny nodded.

"Air what?" Bucktooth wanted to know.

"Airboat," Manny told him. "They use them in swamps. An airplane engine on a plank, practically. No draught. They say they'll float on a heavy dew. I've seen movies of them."

"What's the arrangement when we get there, Manny?" I asked him. I didn't want him thinking I was going too easily. I wanted him unsuspicious.

If I'd ever been in doubt about their plans for me, the glance they exchanged removed it. "A three-way split," Manny said finally. "If it's all there," he amended it. "There's enough for us all." Bucktooth turned his head but not before I saw his ugly grin.

There was only one bed in the room. Bucktooth motioned me to a chair. "Squat, pal," he said to me. He produced a length of manila and efficiently roped me to the chair, my arms to the arms, a leg to each front leg. Manny tested the job, then stretched out on the bed, taking off only his shoes. Bucktooth soon joined him. They left the light on.

The room grew quiet. My head hurt. My ribs hurt. My legs went to sleep. I was uncomfortable, but I wasn't too upset. My time was coming. Daylight would signal the beginning of the end of the line for the two men on the bed.

When I got these two city types out in the swamp, I'd leave them there, permanently.

I must have dozed off eventually, because their stirring around woke me. The light was still on, but at the edges of the curtains I could see early morning sunshine. "Where do we get the airboat?" Manny asked me while Bucktooth was unwinding the rope from around me.

"We rent it. There's a place about seven miles east on Main Street." My arms weren't in bad shape after the night in the chair, but I couldn't stand up. I massaged my legs. It was ten minutes before I could walk. Bucktooth glowered impatiently while I hobbled around.

As soon as we got outside I could tell from the sun and the haze it was going to be a hot, humid day, a real stinger. So much the better. East of the traffic light in town we stopped for breakfast. They took turns going in while one stayed in the station wagon with me. Manny brought me out coffee and a sweet roll.

Out beyond the edge of town I didn't have to say a word. Manny saw the shack with the hand-painted sign "Airboat For Hire" I'd noticed my first day in Hudson. He pulled the wagon in under a tree. "Bring him on down when I signal you," he said to Bucktooth, and walked down to a little dock. We could see him talking to a slatternly looking woman, and in a couple of minutes a boy hand-poled an airboat up to the dock from around behind the shack. Manny raised his arm.

"We won't need any conversation," Bucktooth said, nudging me. We went down the path. I could see Bucktooth looking distrustfully at the wide-planked, battered hull with its high, platform seats, and the big propeller encased in wire mesh. Three or four of the planks were fresh where someone had ripped out the bottom on a snag.

I stepped up onto the boat and started the engine. It was an old type with a hand throttle and a rudimentary tiller. I revved it a few times, listening, then slowed it down and tested the plugs and the battery. I checked the gas gauge and the compass. I had no intention of being left high and wet in the swamp myself.

When the kid who'd brought the boat around saw I knew what I was doing, he wandered off back to the shack. The woman had already disappeared. "Can't you run this thing?" Bucktooth demanded of Manny when the kid left. "I don't like him runnin' it."

"I can run it," Manny said. I knew he couldn't from the way he said it. "He's the one who's got to find the right spot, though. Just keep an eye on him."

He climbed up into one of the front platform seats. Bucktooth settled himself in the dishpan cockpit, facing me, his back braced against a platform strut. He could watch every move I made in the navigator's bucket seat. "You'll get wet down there," I said.

"Just you see to it I don't get wet, pal," he answered me. I would have preferred them in reversed positions. Manny had the keys to the wagon, and my Smith & Wesson. "How long's this going to take us?"

I shrugged. "Hour and a half each way." It wasn't going to take a third of that if I had my way.

I eased away from the dock. Bucktooth stared nervously at the brackish water lapping the boat's low sides. Up on the platform I could see Manny flinch the first few times I rammed the boat over deceptively solid-looking areas of saw-grass.

The sun beat down on us. In no time there were black patches of perspiration on Manny's back and under his arms. Bucktooth was sweating freely, too. Under the gnarled cypress trees with their trailing moss there was shade but no coolness. The swamp was a miasma of sticky heat. I turned right and left through wide channels, enough to get them thoroughly confused. I kept an eye on the compass, and an eye out for mangrove roots that might have tipped us over or stove in a plank. Beneath the thick, green jungle growth overhead the engine didn't sound as noisy. Mosquitoes and gnats hummed around us. Manny and Bucktooth swatted busily. My hide is tougher. Once or twice Manny turned to look back at me. I could see that for the first time he was beginning to have doubts about the expedition.

I gave them enough time to get relaxed, then began watching for a wide-enough space between the trees off the channel accompanied by a low-lying branch of the right height. I passed up a couple that didn't look exactly like what I wanted.

When I saw one that did, I didn't wait any longer.

The tree-opening was on the left, more than wide enough to slip the boat into. "Alligator!" I yelled, and pointed to the right.

"Where?" They bellowed it together. Bucktooth turned in the direction I pointed. Manny stood up to look. I slammed the throttle wide open and aimed hard left. The boat stood up on its port gunwale as it darted between the trees. The low-lying branch caught Manny in the chest. He went off the platform like an ice cube from a spilled cocktail glass. He sling-shotted into the tree on the right. Even above the engine roar I could hear the splash he made as he hit the mud below.

With the tiller hard right and two thirds of the way around the first tree I shut the engine off. Bucktooth had grabbed with both hands to save himself from sliding overboard, and I reached down and slipped the little .17 caliber out of its shin holster. As we drifted back out into the main channel, Bucktooth started to turn to check on the shut-off engine. "Don't turn a thing but your head, man," I told him, my voice loud in the sudden quiet. Looking over his shoulder, he turned white when he saw what I had in my hand.

Desperately he looked up at the platform for Manny. His gaze sped then to the space between the trees, and his eyes bugged out at the sight of Manny in the mud, only his legs visible above the greenish water. The legs were kicking feebly.

"Drop your gun in the water," I directed him. I didn't even blink while he did it. I needn't have worried. His nerve was gone. He was ashen, and his hands were shaking. He was a long way removed from the gun-toting bully who'd taken so much pleasure in pushing me around last night. "You don't deserve it, but I'll give you a choice," I said. "I was going to leave you out here, with the heat and the mosquitoes and the bugs and the snakes and the alligators. You'll never make it in. I doubt if I could myself." His whole face was wet as he stared at me. "You won't go easy if you stay, so I'll give you the choice. Stay, or take one dead center from this." I waved the little handgun.

He couldn't speak at all for a second. "You'd—you'd shoot me?"

I laughed. "What the hell were you planning to do to me? Come on, make up your mind. Which is it going to be?" His eyes darted wildly in all directions. "Take the bullet," I said. "You'll go out of your mind out here in twelve hours." His chest was heaving as he tried to pump air through his constricted throat. "Take the bullet."

"No!" It was wrenched from him forcibly.

"Okay." I ruddered the boat over to a little saw-grass island with one half-grown scotch pine slanting up out of it. "Jump."

"Listen, you wouldn't—"

"Jump, you bastard. Or catch the bullet."

I moved my arm. He jumped. He shrieked as he went in up to his knees in the gelid ooze. He grabbed at the tree, and yelled again as something slithered away under his hands. He kept trying to pull his legs up out of the muck.

I started the engine and turned the boat around. The last I saw of him he was halfway up into the tree that was doubling over under his weight. If he was making any noise I couldn't hear him over the engine.

I went back to Manny Sebastian. His legs were under water now, too. I had a hell of a time pulling him far enough up out of the mud to get my Smith & Wesson out of his pants. I didn't bother with the keys to the wagon. I dropped him back in. If it was any consolation to him, I don't think he drowned. His neck was broken.

I rode the compass back to the shack. I poled in the last half mile and beached the airboat three hundred yards beyond the dock, behind a point. As long as the station wagon stayed there for security, the crackers weren't going to worry too much about their boat. By the time they started to I'd be long gone from Hudson.

I walked a mile, then hitched a ride into town. I made and remade plans all the way. I had a date with Lucille for five o'clock. I was through fooling around. Five o'clock was going to be the payoff, but I had a few things to do first.

In town it must have been ninety, but it felt almost chilly compared to the swamp. I went into the truck-stop diner south of the traffic light in the square and had a meal. I could hardly believe it when I looked at my watch and saw it was still only ten thirty in the morning.

I borrowed a sheet of paper, an envelope, and a pencil from the girl cashier. I took a couple of napkins and practiced composing telegraph messages. I finally hit on one I thought would do the trick. ARRIVING SOON MEET ME LAZY SUSAN URGENT YOU NOT FAIL ME. I addressed it to Dick Pierce, General Delivery, Hudson, Florida, and I signed it Roy.

I copied it out on the sheet of paper and sealed it up in the envelope along with two one-dollar bills. On the outside of the envelope I printed "Western Union." I sat there in the diner by the window watching the northbound, over-the-road, diesel-rigged, big vans pull into the yard, and I watched the drivers as they came in and sat down at the counter.

When a likely-looking middle-aged man came in off a furniture rig, I gave him a five-dollar bill and the envelope and asked him to drop it off at the Western Union office wherever he was at noontime. He said he'd be sure to do it. I sat there till he pulled out of the yard and up the road.

When that message hit the deck in the Hudson Western Union office it would be sent around to the post office and delivered to Lucille Grimes. When it was I should get a little action for my seven dollars. The telegram with that signature should give Lucille Grimes and Blaze Franklin something to think about besides Chet Arnold.

I walked from the diner to the motel. Inside I took the phone off the hook. If Jed was trying to call me about Kaiser, better he should think the line was busy than that he couldn't reach me. I took out the Smith & Wesson and I spent thirty minutes cleaning, oiling, and completely refurbishing it. Then I got into the shower and did the same for myself.

At noon I was back uptown and parked across the street from the post office. Through the big front window I had a good view of the General Delivery window. The alphabetized slots were right behind the window. I'd specified noon for the sending of the telegram because from twelve to two Lucille was in the post office with just one clerk, and almost always handled the front herself.

I spread a newspaper over the steering wheel, and settled down to wait. I could feel the pressure building up. I don't have nerves, but I get keyed up. Everything around me is magnified a couple of dozen times, including the tick of a watch and the color of the sky.

It was hot in the car, even with the windows down, but not as hot as where I'd just come from. Not as hot as plowing up and down half-grown-over back roads on the east side of Main, either. I was through with that stuff. This little deal was going to pop the weasel right out of the box.

It was one twenty-five when the Western Union kid rode up on his bike. He kicked it up on its stand and went on inside. I saw him lay the telegram down on the counter, and in a minute Lucille appeared at the window and picked it up and looked at it. She looked at it a long time. I could see the kid reminding her she hadn't signed for it.

She scribbled her name, and the kid went out. She never even looked at the General Delivery slots behind her. Telegram in hand, she made a beeline for the back. Telephone call, I told myself. I folded up my newspaper and laid it on the seat beside me. In three minutes Lucille was at the front door. I could see her explaining something over her shoulder to the clerk she'd moved up to the front window.

She came out and walked hurriedly to a red MG parked three doors down the street. A double-parked delivery van had kept me from noticing it before. She climbed in, backed up, and ripped up the street. I was facing the wrong way. I swung in a wide U and took out after her.

She hightailed it through town, straight north on 19. I dogged her at a distance. I didn't need to stay too close. I knew where she was going. No farther than it took to meet Blaze Franklin, Deputy Sheriff, in some kind of privacy.

Actually they didn't bother too much about the privacy. From a quarter-mile behind her I watched her pull off onto the shoulder of the road. She tucked the red MG right in on the tail of a two-tone county cruiser. Blaze Franklin's thick-bodied figure was out of the cruiser and on the way over to the MG before its wheels had stopped rolling.

From a curve away I had no trouble at all in seeing his red face and the yellow flash of the telegram as he snatched it away from her and tore it open. She'd been afraid to open it herself, evidently.

Franklin climbed into the MG beside her. Their heads stayed close together for what seemed like fifteen minutes. I'd have given a quarter to be a fly on the windshield during that conversation. When Franklin jumped out of the MG and headed for the cruiser, I was ready. I swung around and headed back to town. At the first intersection I turned off and parked. In less than a minute the cruiser came flying down the highway, its siren rrr'ing. Franklin was hunched over the wheel, his tomato face like a bulldog's.

Three minutes later the MG came by. Lucille's face was white and strained-looking.

I followed along behind.

Curtain going up.

When I walked into the office of the Lazy Susan two hours later, Blaze Franklin was cocked up against the wall in a straight-backed chair, big as life and twice as nasty. If it had been me that's where I'd have been, too, but I still had to grade him A for nerve.

After the first quick look when I came in the door he paid no attention. Mr. Franklin had other things on his mind now than Chet Arnold. They had to figure now they'd had me in the wrong picture. I asked at the desk for mail, not that there ever was any. The young clerk behind the desk tried to engage Blaze in conversation after he'd finished with me. Franklin bit his head off neatly in about eight well-chosen words. The kid turned a dull red and subsided.

I went out and walked down to my unit. From it I could see the office, and I could see Franklin. Twice in the first few minutes he got up and picked up the phone on the desk without a by-your-leave and made a call. It suited me fine. The longer he sat there the more things he could think of to go wrong. I wanted him shook. I hoped the phone calls were to Lucille. I wanted her shook.

Most of all I wanted Franklin right where he was. His uniform made it hard for me to move openly against him. I could kill them both, but that wouldn't get me the bundle. As long as Franklin was nailed down here, I could be sure of getting to Lucille with no interruptions. And if she gave me a hard time about where the bundle was, I'd shake her till she atomized.

I watched him off and on for another hour. He made a couple of more phone calls. He was a busy boy. At four fifteen I shaved and started to change for my date with Lucille. Buttoning my shirt, I went back to the window. I couldn't see Franklin. I could see the chair he'd been in, but he wasn't in it. I waited a couple of minutes. Wherever he was, he didn't come back.

I finished dressing in a hurry. I shoved the .38 in its holster, slipped into my jacket, and crossed over to the office. In the first quick look around I could see Franklin wasn't anywhere inside. I looked at the clerk. "The bird dog gone?"

He didn't spit, but he almost did. "Good riddance."

"He say where he could be reached?"

"He said nothin'."

"He get a call from anyone?"

The kid shook his head. "He made enough of 'em, though. The last one he swore an' banged up the receiver an' took off."

I went outside and sat in the Ford. What in the hell had happened? Nothing on earth should have moved Blaze Franklin out of that chair. That telegram from Roy Martin should have made him afraid to move. He should have sat there, getting madder and shakier by the minute. That telegram should have immobilized him.

He must have seen that his only chance of keeping the lid on—once he read the telegram—was to intercept Roy Martin, and dispose of him quietly. Nothing should have been able to move Franklin away from that motel office.

I went back over it step by step. Gradually the only logical answer forced itself on me. I'd underrated the sonofabitch. Suppose he'd been smart enough to call the point of origin of the telegram and ask for a description of the sender? Once he knew the circumstances under which it had been sent he was right back in the saddle. With the telegram exposed as a phony, how much brains did he need to figure out who'd sent it up the road to have it bounce back here off his noggin?

So why hadn't he rushed into my motel unit and shot me up, down, and sideways and triumphantly hauled in the riddled corpse? It was exactly what he should have done. If he had the sense to short-circuit the boobytrap I'd set up for him, how could he have missed the obvious follow-up?

There was something I didn't understand.

Something I didn't know.

It was time I learned it.

I started up the Ford. Nothing was changed, really, except that I had to keep an eye peeled for Franklin.

I drove up to the post office to collect Lucille.

She was standing out on the sidewalk when I pulled up in front. I opened the door and she got in. "Let's stop for a drink at the Dixie Pig first, shall we?" she said without any preliminary greeting at all.

My first impulse was to refuse. In the first place I didn't want to wave this long-legged blonde under Hazel's nose. I sneaked a glance at Lucille as she sat beside me, eyes straight ahead. She looked and sounded as brittle as glass. She might as well have worn a sign; whatever had pulled Franklin away from the motel, she knew about. The Dixie Pig was now just another gambit in the game.

Okay. We'd go to the Dixie Pig.

But not together. I drew up in front, reached across her and opened the door again. "You go on in. I just remembered I'm supposed to pick up a few dollars a guy owes me. I'll be back in ten minutes."

She didn't like it, but what could she do? She climbed out reluctantly and closed the door. "Hurry back," she said with an attempt at a smile. The shark's teeth were polished to a high gloss.

I circled the Dixie Pig driveway, and saw right away the hunch had paid off. Snuggled in among the six or eight parked cars was Franklin's cruiser. It had to be Franklin's.

That's why she'd brought me here, so that he could without difficulty take up the trail for what they both felt would be the final act of the drama.

I pulled out on the highway again and in half a mile found a shiftless-looking country grocery. I stopped in and bought two pounds of brown sugar. Back in the Ford I opened it and set it down carefully on the seat beside me. I drove back to the Dixie Pig and around to the back parking lot. There was a hole two parking spaces away from the cruiser. I nosed into it.

I sat there, watching the two windows that looked out on the back parking lot. I couldn't see anyone in either booth. I picked up the sugar, got out of the Ford, walked around the rear of the car between it and the cruiser, removed the cruiser's gas cap, dumped in the brown sugar, slapped the cap back on, and crushed the bag and stuffed it in my pocket. It might have taken me six seconds. The sugar I spilled was indistinguishable on the crushed stone.

I brushed off my hands and walked in the Dixie Pig's back door. If they'd seen me drive in, I was right on schedule.

Franklin sat at the bar, his back elaborately to the door through which I'd entered. Lucille bounced up from a booth, so quickly she had to have seen me drive in. She met me in the center of the floor. "I don't think I feel like a drink right now, after all, Chet. Couldn't we wait till we eat?"

"Anything you say," I told her. We turned to the door. It was a rush act of superb proportions. I hadn't been in the place thirty seconds, but Franklin was already gone from the bar, ready to take up the pursuit in the cruiser. Behind the bar Hazel all but stood on her head trying to attract my attention. I avoided looking at her as we went out.

The cruiser was gone. Franklin would pick us up on the highway. How would he know whether to go north or south? I found out how he knew. "There's a new restaurant south on the highway, Chet. If you're feeling experimental, I understand it's quite good."

"Anything you say," I repeated. Full twilight wasn't many minutes away when I ran back down the driveway and out onto the highway. "How far is this place?"

"Oh, a dozen to fifteen miles. It's supposed to be quite

attractive." Her voice was as cool as a mountain brook. Only the hands clenched in her lap betrayed her inner tension.

Fifteen miles was the superlative of fine. Franklin shouldn't be able to fetch half that before the sugar in his gas line froze his engine down tight. It was a bonus that he'd be decommissioned outside of town.

South of the square I switched on my lights. I watched the shoulder of the road. About a mile beyond we passed a car pulled off on the right, almost indistinguishable in the gathering darkness. If I hadn't been looking for it, I never would have seen it. In the rear-view mirror I watched its parking lights come on as it rolled out on the highway behind us. The wolf was in the sheep-fold. We played follow-the-leader down U.S. 19 in the deepening twilight.

He dogged me from so far back I couldn't be sure where I'd lost him, or if I actually had. He hadn't needed to stay too close because he knew where we were going. After a few miles there were no lights of any kind behind me. I didn't think even Franklin would be running that letter-S stretch without them.

It was a silent ride. Each of us was busy with private thoughts. Lucille roused herself when we'd been on the road about twenty minutes. "You'll have to watch for the turnoff," she said, leaning forward in the seat. "There's a big white sign, and then it's off to the left about a mile."

Naturally they wanted a place not on the main highway. We both saw the sign at the same time. I was already slowing down when Lucille pointed. I turned into a graveled side road at eight miles an hour. No lights of any kind turned in behind us.

A half mile in a wagon-road branched off in the headlights. I turned up it. "Not that way!" Lucille said sharply. I paid no attention. I went up it about fifty yards, pulled up the brake, and cut the motor and lights. Insurance in case a raging Franklin again proved himself shrewder than I'd anticipated and succeeded in commandeering another car.

"Plenty of time for food," I said to Lucille, and slipped an arm around her. My purpose was to keep her from fleeing if she suspected anything. She didn't. She humored me to the extent of lowering her head on my shoulder. She was content to await the arrival of the rear guard. It was full dark under the trees.

I wished I could see her face. It would have interested me to be able to read her expression. As far as I was concerned, Lucille Grimes was already dead. It was just a question of when, and how. In a way it was too bad. This was a really talented bitch.

Right that second she gave me a demonstration of it. She grabbed the horn ring on the steering wheel. The horn blatted twice. She was reaching for the lights when I caught her arm. She sat there tensely with her arm in my grip, waiting for Blaze Franklin to come up out of the darkness and kill me.

I could sense the shriveling of her self-confidence when nothing happened. "You beginning to get the idea he's not coming?" I asked her. "He's not splitting with you, Lucille. He's splitting with me. Your boyfriend's sold you out. I'm supposed to bury you twenty yards off this side road."

It shook her to her heels, but she was too smart to go for it completely. "He'll kill you," she croaked. She tried to look over her shoulder.

"Where is he, then?" I needled her. "Get smart, woman. It's lucky for you I like you. Now get on the ball and steer me to the money. I'll take care of Franklin for you."

There was only one thing she could think. Even if Franklin hadn't sold her out, if he'd flubbed his end of the deal she had to protect herself. She knew who I was, and she knew there was no reason on earth I shouldn't leave her body in the bushes beside the car. Her steel-trap mind should have been telling her she was in perfect position to play it cool right down to the finish line, and then choose up sides with the winner.

I couldn't understand why she hesitated so long.

"We—we never found the money," she said at last. Her voice was husky. "Only the thousand in the envelope and a few thousand on—on him." She drew a quivering breath. "If only I'd never mentioned to Blaze the big, odd-looking man who mailed such queer—" Her voice died away.

So that was why Franklin wanted me alive. He hoped I knew where the bundle was. The funny part of it was, I did. Now.

I tightened the grip on her arm. "Franklin killed him before he found out where the money was?"

"He—yes," she whispered.

So Franklin hadn't been able to crack Bunny. I started up the Ford. "Tell me where he was staying, Lucille." She was silent. I turned my head to look at her. Her face was just an indistinct pale oval. "Tell me," I warned her. "Franklin might not have been able to find it, but I'll find it."

She told me. She had trouble getting it out. The directions would have put Bunny's place north of town. I pulled on the dash light. She was watching me, and she backed off as far as she could go. I crossed my hand over my chest and drew the Smith & Wesson. Her face crumpled with fear. I took hold of her and pulled her toward me, reversed the gun, and slashed her across her soft inner arm with the front gunsight. She cried out in pain and shock as the blood welled. "I'm giving you a chance to change that story," I told her. "Because if we get where you send me and there's nothing there, that's what happens to your face till my arm gets tired."

She changed the story.

The new one put Bunny's place east of town, which sounded a lot better to me.

I got out of there. Lucille sat huddled in the seat beside me. I hadn't expected her to go to pieces so completely. The way I'd sized her up she should have had no trouble at all riding with a foot on each saddle till either Franklin or I got dumped. She must be scared to death of Franklin.

We were on the right side of town but it still took us nearly an hour to get there. I had a funny feeling riding east on Main past the shack with the sign out in front, "Airboat For Hire." The side road Lucille reluctantly directed me up couldn't have been more than a couple of miles beyond the point where I'd been so painfully slogging over brambled trails. No wonder Franklin had been getting itchy.

It was a small cabin way out in the middle of nowhere. I got out of the Ford and ran a flashlight around the building. No telephone wires. Fine. I circled it cautiously. In the rear a mound of cut branches loomed up in the light. I pulled off a couple. There sat the blue Dodge, up on blocks.

So Lucille hadn't lied to me. I returned to the Ford. She still sat in it, motionless. I had to take her by the arm again to get her out. She didn't want to come with me.

I got a chisel and maul out of the trunk of the Ford, herded Lucille up to the door ahead of me, and broke the lock. A wave of dry heat rolled out at me as it opened, a musty, long-closed smell. I wondered if this was the right place, after all. I kept a good hold on Lucille's arm.

Inside I closed the door and stationed her away from it. I walked through the place. A skillet was still on the two-burner stove. Bunny's clothes hung neatly on hangers. There were two more locked doors. A couple of swings of the maul disposed of both. There was nothing at all in the first room. I beamed the flash rapidly around the interior of the second one, and then it hung there, motionless.

I'd found Bunny.

He was face down on the rough pine flooring. His wrists were handcuffed to ringbolts in the floor at right angles to his head. The ringbolts were new. Fresh pine sawdust was still visible where the holes had been drilled for them.

Dry as the air in the place was there was another odor. Bunny had been in the cuffs a long time. With his chest flat on the floor and his arms spread-eagled, not even his great strength could achieve leverage. In a final contortion he had thrown himself onto his right side. The bone of his left knee glistened at me out of raw-looking meat, the trousers and flesh long since abraded away in his ceaseless struggle with the flooring. His upper left arm was mincemeat where he'd gnawed at himself.

He'd lain in the cuffs till he died.

Which kills first, hunger or thirst? I couldn't remember. I couldn't think.

The game had dealt Bunny a tough hand. Looking into Franklin's gun, he must have temporized, thinking he'd find a spot to turn it around. He hadn't counted on the cuffs. He'd gone into them, but he hadn't cracked. How do you break a stubborn man? You starve him. When he's out of his mind with hunger and thirst, he'll lead you to anything he has.

If he's not too far out of his mind. With the hunger, the thirst, and the maddening heat, Franklin had returned to the cabin one day and found a mindless animal that could never lead him to anything.

I stooped and examined the head, cruelly battered from endless, raving contact with the floor. There had been no merciful bullet.

Franklin had left him to die.

Franklin and Lucille Grimes had left him to die.

I knew now why she'd been so afraid to come in here with me. She'd known exactly what I was going to find.

I straightened up and drew the Smith & Wesson. I walked out into the other room.

"Blaze did it!" she screamed when she saw my face. "Blaze did it! I wanted to let him—"

I shot her in the throat, three times.

"Tell your story in hell, if you can get anyone to listen," I told her. She thrashed on the floor, blood pulsing between the fingers of the hands clasped to her neck. "If they can patch up your lying voice."

I stepped over her. I had work to do.

I went outside, into the clean darkness. I looked up at the stars to orient myself. I knew where the sack would be. For a cache out in the country, Bunny and I had always followed a pattern. From the front door of the cabin I stepped out due north as accurately as I could figure it. I knew it wouldn't be more than thirty or forty feet from the cabin.

In the daylight it would have been a cinch, and even in the dark it wasn't hard. My feet told me as soon as I hit softer earth. Bunny had planted something green over it. I ripped it up, pulled the chisel out of my pocket that was the only tool I had, and tore into the loose ground. A foot below the surface I ran into the sack.

I hauled it up and by the light of the flash made certain that the bulk of the swag was still in it. Then I reburied it, stamping down the earth. No sense lugging it around with me. I'd be back for it. I'd be back for it when I brought Blaze Franklin out here and roped him down to Bunny's body and left him to die in the same way he'd left Bunny.

I went back inside for a look around. Lucille was unconscious. Bubbles of blood pulsed gently now instead of jetting with each ragged breath. She wouldn't last long. She was lucky. If I hadn't been so mad that I hadn't stopped to think, I could have figured a different end for her. She was just as guilty as Franklin.

Death I'm used to, but Bunny's infuriated me. Where would Franklin be now? Back at the Lazy Susan, probably, chewing up the rug. He had to hope I came back there. He'd get his wish in a way he never expected.

I went back out to the Ford and got out of there.

I drove straight to the Dixie Pig. I wanted Franklin so bad I could taste it, but I had another errand first. I scouted the back parking lot carefully. No two-tone cruiser. I parked beside Hazel's car and went on in.

Hazel was behind the bar that had a half-dozen customers. Her face lighted up when she saw me. She made a circling motion with her hand that beckoned me behind the bar, and held up the hinged flap at the far end. I walked on in and out through the hanging curtain in the center of the back-bar. I'd never been out there before. It was set up as a lounging room, with a couch and a couple of chairs, a Primus stove and a coffeepot.

"Get a bag packed," I said to her when she came through the curtain behind me. "I'll be back for you in an hour."

Her big hand caught mine and squeezed it, hard. "Listen to me, Chet. Please." Her voice was low and intense. "Franklin has everyone out looking for you. There's half a dozen of them waiting for you down in the motel yard. They never dreamed you'd come back here."

So. End of the line in Hudson, Florida. And I couldn't get Franklin. I couldn't? The hell I couldn't. I held out my hand to Hazel. "Forget what I said about a bag. Give me your car keys."

She turned to her handbag on a chair. "Chet, please let me come—"

"Tell them I took the keys away from you," I cut her off. I couldn't take her with me now. I was something less than even money to make it. "Forget what I said about packing a bag." She handed me the keys. "Tell them I took—" I shut myself off. I was starting to repeat myself. I punched Hazel in the eye. Big as she was she went over backward and landed on the couch. The eye would be her alibi. "So long, baby," I said from the curtained opening. I didn't look back. I didn't want to see the expression on her face.

I drove down to the motel in her car. They should have been looking for my Ford. It turned out they were looking for anything. I'd no more than rolled into the yard and opened the car door when some eager beaver tapped his headlights. Instantly three more sets came on. I was semi-circled by cruisers. The motel yard looked bright as day.

Blaze Franklin came roaring out of the nearest cruiser, waving a gun. He had to be first. He couldn't let me talk. At ten yards I put five in a row into him a playing card could have covered. He went down, bellowing like a wounded bull. He *was* a wounded bull. A dark red stain spread over the front of his uniform trousers. He'd live. He wouldn't enjoy it. I put the last one into his jaw as he flopped on the ground, to keep him quiet if I made the getaway good.

Firecrackers were going off all around me. They couldn't shoot worth a damn. I dived back in under the wheel and aimed the car straight ahead through the largest gap in the encircling headlights. Gravel spurted. Someone shot out the windshield. I ducked flying glass, bumped over the lawn, through the flower bed, around the swimming pool, and over a white picket fence. I jounced down onto the highway and floored the accelerator. For the first five hundred yards part of the fence kept banging against the front wheels of Hazel's car. Then it fell off.

Behind me were lights and sirens. No shortage of either. I busted right through the square and set sail for the Dixie Pig. In the souped-up Ford I at least had a chance of out-running them. Right now I could just about smell the over-heated engines behind me.

A thousand yards from the Dixie Pig I cut the lights, got over on the shoulder, and drove in darkness. If there had been anything parked out there it would have been Katy-Bar-the-door. I whirled the wheel hard when I saw the lighter outline of the crushed stone driveway. I took a section of hedge with me, but I made the turn. I belted it around to the back. Outside on the highway the cruisers screamed on by.

I yanked up the emergency and lit running. The door on the driver's side of the Ford stood open. I didn't remember leaving it open. I came to a sliding stop beside it, my hand on the butt of my .38 when I saw a dark figure on the other side of the front seat. I came within a tick of blasting it before I recognized Hazel. "Get the hell out of there!" I ordered her, trying to listen for sounds on the highway.

"'Take me with you, Chet,'' she pleaded. "Give me a gun."

"Don't make me do it, baby," I warned her. "Get out of the car."

She got out. I could see she was crying. "Chet—"

"Stop making these losing bets, will you?" I got in under the wheel. "Get back inside and keep your mouth shut." I backed up, swung around, and rammed the Ford down the driveway. The last I saw of Hazel was the glitter of the silver conches on her cowboy boots in the big swing of the headlights.

I doubled back toward town. There were bound to be road blocks north and south on 19. I'd head east, on Main. The added power of the Ford felt good under my foot. I blasted the road. Approaching the traffic light I slowed down. I'd just started to make the left-hand turn when there was the snarl of a siren practically in my ear. Somebody in the posse had had the brains to leave a trailer. He was headed the wrong way, but I saw the shine of his lights as he swung around after me. My forty-five-mile-an-hour turn carried me up onto the sidewalk before I got straightened out on Main.

I really rolled it away from there. I was doing eighty-five on a road built for forty. The Ford was all over the road. I watched the dark ribbon of macadam unroll in the headlights. Behind me the wailing shriek of the siren pierced the night, but I was outrunning him. Then I burst out of a curve into a long straight-away, and far up the road winked the red lights of trouble.

Road block.

Instinctively I lifted my foot off the gas, but I still rolled up on it fast. A spotlight came on when they saw me. A tiny figure stood out in the road, waving me down with flapping arms. I sized it up. Two cruisers across the road, their snouts extending way out onto the shoulders. Three quarters of a car's width between them in the center. Ditch on the right. Open field on the left. And in the rear-view mirror the lights of the trailing cruiser rapidly gaining.

A road block you do or you don't. I mashed down on the gas and headed for the center opening between the end-to-end cruisers. I just might rip my way through. The fool with the flapping arms stood right in the center of the gap. The headlights picked him up solidly. Roaring down on him, I was suddenly looking through the windshield into the white, strained face of Jed Raymond.

I hoped he'd jump. Jed was a nice kid. If he didn't, though, he'd have to take his chances, as I was taking mine. I couldn't have been twenty yards from him—and he hadn't made a move—when Kaiser pranced out in front of him from behind a cruiser, head cocked, tongue lolling, tail waving.

My brain sent me straight on through, over the dog and Jed, to try the odds with the cruisers. But hands spun the wheel, hard left. Somebody else will have to explain it to you. I missed them both, caromed broadside off the left-hand cruiser in a whining, ear-splitting shriek of tortured metal, and hurtled a hundred fifty yards down into the field. The front wheels dropped suddenly into a ditch. There was a loud whump, and the Ford stood up on its nose. The doors flew open. I flew out. I hit hard, and rolled.

I didn't lose consciousness. I still had the gun. The Ford was down on its knees in front, its ass-end up in the air, the wheels still spinning. I started to crawl over to it, and knew in the first second my right leg was broken.

Up on the road the spotlight pivoted and crept down through the field. It caught me, passed on, hesitated, and came back. There was a sharp crack, and a bullet plowed up the ground beside me. Rifle. Sounded like a .30-.30. I crawled over the uneven ground to the Ford, underneath the back wheels where I could see up to the road. I reloaded in a hurry, and got the spotlight with my third shot.

They turned the other cruiser around—the one I hadn't hit—and its spotlight started down through the field. I popped it out before it reached me. Not that it made any difference. More red lights, sirens, and spotlights were whirling up to the roadblock every second now.

I reloaded the Smith & Wesson again. Nothing for it now but the hard sell. Nothing for it but to see to it a few of them shook hands with the devil at the same time I did.

To get me in a hurry they had to come through the field. By now they knew enough not to be in a hurry. The .30-.30

went off again, and a large charge of angry metal whanged through the body of the car over my head. The rifle would keep me pinned down while they circled around behind me.

The spotlights were crisscrossing each other in an eerie pattern in the open field, but one of them had the Ford pinned down steadily. A hump in the ground kept me in shadow. I couldn't see anyone coming through the field.

I heard the rifle's sharp crack again. Above my head there was a loud ping!! Suddenly I was drenched to the waist in gasoline. The .30-.30 slug had ripped out the belly of the gas tank. I swiped at my stinging eyes and shook my dripping head. I looked up just as gas from my hair splashed onto the hot exhaust.

Whoom!!

I saw a bright flare, and then I didn't see anything. The explosion knocked me backward under the car. I rolled out from beneath it. I didn't even feel the broken leg I was dragging. I couldn't see at all. My eyes were gone. I could hear the crackle of flames. Part was the Ford. Part was me. I was afire all over.

I tried to smother the flames on the ground. It didn't help. I still had the gun. I hoped they could see me and were coming at me. I knelt up on my good leg and faced the noise up on the road, bracing the Smith & Wesson in both hands. I squeezed off the whole load, waist-high in a semicircle. I think the last shot exploded in the chamber from the heat of my burning hands. I threw the empty gun as far as I could in the direction of the road.

There was a dull roaring sound in my ears. I tried to put out the fire in my hair. I rolled on the ground. I could smell my own burning flesh.

The last thing I heard was myself, screaming.

I was in black darkness for six months. I may have gone a little crazy, too. I gave them a hard time. I went the whole route: baths, wet packs, elbow cuffs, straightjackets, isolation. I stopped fighting them a little while ago. They don't pay much attention to me now.

Even before I could see again, I knew what I looked like. I could feel the reaction, when a new patient was admitted, or a new attendant came on duty. Hazel came to see me four or five times. I refused permission for her to be allowed in.

They don't know that I can see again, that I'm not crazy. They think I'm a robot. A vegetable.

I'll show them.

I have a hermetically sealed quart jar buried in the ground up in Hillsboro, New Hampshire, and another in Grosmont, Colorado, up above timber line. There's nothing but money in both. I don't need it. All I need is a gun. Some one of these days I'll find the right attendant, and I'll start talking to him. It will take a while to convince him, but I've got plenty of time.

If I can get back to the sack buried beside Bunny's cabin, plastic surgery will take care of most of what I look like. With a gun, I'll get back to it.

That's all I need—a gun.

I'm not staying here.

I'll be leaving one of these days, and the day I do they'll never forget it.

THE END

VINTAGE CRIME / BLACK LIZARD

___ **Carny Kill** by Robert Edmond Alter	$8.00	0-679-74443-6
___ **Swamp Sister** by Robert Edmond Alter	$9.00	0-679-74442-8
___ **The Far Cry** by Fredric Brown	$8.00	0-679-73469-4
___ **His Name Was Death** by Fredric Brown	$8.00	0-679-73468-6
___ **No Beast So Fierce** by Edward Bunker	$10.00	0-679-74155-0
___ **Double Indemnity** by James M. Cain	$8.00	0-679-72322-6
___ **The Postman Always Rings Twice** by James M. Cain	$8.00	0-679-72325-0
___ **The Big Sleep** by Raymond Chandler	$9.00	0-394-75828-5
___ **Farewell, My Lovely** by Raymond Chandler	$10.00	0-394-75827-7
___ **The High Window** by Raymond Chandler	$10.00	0-394-75826-9
___ **The Lady in the Lake** by Raymond Chandler	$10.00	0-394-75825-0
___ **The Long Goodbye** by Raymond Chandler	$10.00	0-394-75768-8
___ **Trouble Is My Business** by Raymond Chandler	$9.00	0-394-75764-5
___ **I Wake Up Screaming** by Steve Fisher	$8.00	0-679-73677-8
___ **Black Friday** by David Goodis	$7.95	0-679-73255-1
___ **The Burglar** by David Goodis	$8.00	0-679-73472-4
___ **Cassidy's Girl** by David Goodis	$8.00	0-679-73851-7
___ **Night Squad** by David Goodis	$8.00	0-679-73698-0
___ **Nightfall** by David Goodis	$8.00	0-679-73474-0
___ **Shoot the Piano Player** by David Goodis	$7.95	0-679-73254-3
___ **Street of No Return** by David Goodis	$8.00	0-679-73473-2
___ **The Continental OP** by Dashiell Hammett	$10.00	0-679-72258-0
___ **The Maltese Falcon** by Dashiell Hammett	$9.00	0-679-72264-5
___ **Red Harvest** by Dashiell Hammett	$9.00	0-679-72261-0
___ **The Thin Man** by Dashiell Hammett	$9.00	0-679-72263-7
___ **Ripley Under Ground** by Patricia Highsmith	$10.00	0-679-74230-1

VINTAGE CRIME / **BLACK LIZARD**

___ **The Talented Mr. Ripley** by Patricia Highsmith	$10.00	0-679-74229-8
___ **A Rage in Harlem** by Chester Himes	$8.00	0-679-72040-5
___ **Shattered** by Richard Neely	$9.00	0-679-73498-8
___ **The Laughing Policeman** by Maj Sjöwall and Per Wahlöö	$9.00	0-679-74223-9
___ **The Locked Room** by Maj Sjöwall and Per Wahlöö	$10.00	0-679-74222-0
___ **After Dark, My Sweet** by Jim Thompson	$7.95	0-679-73247-0
___ **The Alcoholics** by Jim Thompson	$8.00	0-679-73313-2
___ **The Criminal** by Jim Thompson	$8.00	0-679-73314-0
___ **Cropper's Cabin** by Jim Thompson	$8.00	0-679-73315-9
___ **The Getaway** by Jim Thompson	$8.95	0-679-73250-0
___ **The Grifters** by Jim Thompson	$8.95	0-679-73248-9
___ **A Hell of a Woman** by Jim Thompson	$10.00	0-679-73251-9
___ **The Killer Inside Me** by Jim Thompson	$9.00	0-679-73397-3
___ **Nothing More Than Murder** by Jim Thompson	$9.00	0-679-73309-4
___ **Pop. 1280** by Jim Thompson	$9.00	0-679-73249-7
___ **Recoil** by Jim Thompson	$8.00	0-679-73308-6
___ **Savage Night** by Jim Thompson	$8.00	0-679-73310-8
___ **A Swell-Looking Babe** by Jim Thompson	$8.00	0-679-73311-6
___ **Wild Town** by Jim Thompson	$9.00	0-679-73312-4
___ **The Burnt Orange Heresy** by Charles Willeford	$7.95	0-679-73252-7
___ **Cockfighter** by Charles Willeford	$9.00	0-679-73471-6
___ **Pick-Up** by Charles Willeford	$7.95	0-679-73253-5
___ **The Hot Spot** by Charles Williams	$8.95	0-679-73329-9

Available at your bookstore or call toll-free to order: 1-800-733-3000.
Credit cards only. Prices subject to change.